The Big House

The Big House

Carolyn Coman

DRAWINGS BY
Rob Shepperson

FRONT STREET
Asheville, North Carolina

Text copyright © 2004 by Carolyn Coman
Illustrations copyright © 2004 by Rob Shepperson
Printed in China
All rights reserved
Designed by Helen Robinson
First edition

Library of Congress Cataloging-in-Publication Data

Coman, Carolyn.
The big house / Carolyn Coman; pictures by Rob Shepperson.—1st ed.
p. cm.
Summary: When Ivy and Ray's parents are sent to jail and they are left
in the custody of their parents' accusers, they decide to look
for evidence that will "spring" their parents.
ISBN 1-932425-09-8
[1. Brothers and sisters—Fiction.
2. Crime—Fiction. 3. Humorous stories.]
I. Shepperson, Rob, ill. II. Title
PZ7.C729Bi2004

[Fic]-dc22   2004040425

In loving memory of my brother, Larry,
and how we played.
And for David, who dared me.
C.C.

For Mark and Lisa.
R.S.

The Big House

Contents

The Punishment

The verdict was in.

Ivy watched as her parents, Dan and Carol Fitts, who were on trial for embezzling thousands and thousands of dollars from the estate of Blackstone Mouton, stood to face the judge. She had a perfect view of her father's black curls, so shiny they looked wet, and her mother's perfect curls, red. Ivy's brother, Ray, sat close by her side. No one breathed. Then came the verdict—*guilty*—sailing out and filling up the entire courtroom. *Guilty!*

Ivy jumped to her feet, outraged. "No!" she cried out.

Up until that moment, throughout the whole long trial, Ivy had sat as quiet and still as she knew how to

be. Her parents' lawyer had told Ray and her to act like they were in church (not particularly helpful advice, since they had never been to church), and Ivy and Ray had tried their best. So much for good behavior, Ivy thought once the verdict was announced. It didn't amount to a hill of beans. Dan and Carol had been found guilty.

"You're *wrong*," she called out to the court, and stamped her foot.

"Order!" the judge barked, "order in the court!" and

pounded his hammer on its hammering block. The hammer made a sound that started and stopped everything, and it reverberated throughout the imposing, polished courtroom, straight up Ivy's backbone, and out the top of her head. All during the trial she had wished for a fancy hammer of her own, and now she wanted one more than ever—something *she* could lift and lower to decree what was what. Her hand tightened in a fist at just the thought of wielding one.

Ray tugged at her sleeve and pulled her back down beside him. She crossed her arms hard across her chest and leaned over to him. "It's not fair," she whispered, loud. "It's *not*."

Ivy was sure. She had paid close attention during the trial; she had even kind of enjoyed it, safe in her conviction that her parents would beat the rap. She liked hearing people tell the same story in completely different ways, and she liked deciding who she believed and who she didn't. And she hadn't believed one word Marietta Noland had said about Dan and Carol. The old witch insisted they had embezzled money from the estate of her "dear departed father, Blackstone Mouton," and his charity, the Last, Best Hope.

So how, Ivy wondered, could the judge and jury

possibly have believed Marietta over Dan? Her father's story had been *ten times* better! And he was so much nicer to look at and listen to as he told it, sitting in the chair below and to the side of the judge, explaining how Marietta had recruited him to set up a charity for distributing part of her father's vast fortune. Didn't the judge see how her father had an answer for *everything*? Didn't he notice how beautiful his smile was? Ivy thought the lawyer should have asked Dan to do some of his tricks—hide a pea under walnut shells, know without fail which card you had pulled from the deck, produce a penny from behind your ear—but all anyone had talked about was money. Money, money, money—and who had done what with it.

When Marietta Noland testified, she had worn white gloves with lacy cuffs, and a charm bracelet laden with little things that jiggled whenever she moved her hand, and a hat with fake berries tied around the brim. She had sniffed as she told the story of how Dan Fitts—*that man*, she said in her quavery voice, pointing at Ray and Ivy's father with her bony, crooked finger—had secretly siphoned off thousands of dollars—*untold* thousands, she said. Money her dear father intended for charity!

And the judge had believed *her*, the witch! Ivy

should have known he would: she had distrusted the
judge from day one, from the moment he had entered
the courtroom through the special door in the corner,
his black robe swirling around him. Maybe it was the
mustache. But she also hadn't liked how often he called

the lawyers up to his desk and whispered things that
no one else was allowed to hear.

Now he had declared Dan and Carol guilty. Ivy

knew her parents were in for it. Her father had told her that if the judge got the chance he'd throw the book at them.

Ivy sat up straight. She scanned the judge's desk, set high upon a raised platform. He had his hammer, but she didn't see any book.

And then he spoke. "I sentence you," he began— Ivy closed her eyes tight, but even in the dark of her eyelids she saw a big, fat book sailing straight toward them all—"to twenty-five years."

Ivy was on her feet in a flash, eyes wide. "Twenty-five!" she cried out. Shouting the number only made it explode more inside her head, all those years and years and years and years.

Ray was pulling on her arm again. "What, Ivy—?" he said.

Ivy turned and looked into her little brother's face, a face remarkably like her own. "Forever," she said. It had hit her. "*Both* of them." Dan and Carol had been sent off to jail before, but never at the same time, and never forever!

The entire courtroom was buzzing and stirring. The backs of her parents' heads seemed miles away, all their perfect curls.

The judge pounded his hammer and continued on. Ivy caught only a word now and then. It was roaring between her ears. Finally, little by little, she began to hear again. He was talking about *the children,* and it took her a moment to realize he meant them—Ray and Ivy—and then she had to hurry inside her head to catch up with what he was saying. During the confinement of Dan and Carol Fitts, he droned, their children, as the first beneficiaries of Blackstone Mouton's Last, Best Hope Charity, would be commended to the care of Marietta and Lionel Noland.

Marietta and Lionel! Was he *crazy?* The ones who had accused her parents of embezzlement?

"Generous and forgiving to a fault," said the judge, describing Marietta.

But Marietta and Lionel were the reason Dan and Carol were *going* to jail. Why would Ray and Ivy live with *them?* Who said so? Did they have to?

Thwack! The hammer went down.

The Big House

Carol and Dan's parting words to their children, as they were being led off to jail, were these: Carol whispered to Ivy, "Watch your brother's back." And when Ivy hissed to her father that it wasn't fair, Dan Fitts shrugged and told her, "Looks like we met our match with that old witch, Marietta." And then they were gone, led out the back way, off for more years than Ivy could imagine.

Ivy and Ray were instantly surrounded by a cluster of grownups they didn't know, all of whom parted as Marietta and Lionel, her ancient husband, made their way from the opposite side of the courtroom (where everyone who had been against them had sat). Ivy felt

a light, clawlike hand on her shoulder and turned to look up into Marietta's leathery face.

"Child," the old woman began. She said it like it was a dirty word. "Please accept our hospitality while your parents"—she paused and gave a ghastly smile—"pay their debt to society."

Ivy remembered that the lawyer had called Marietta and Lionel pillars of society. Lionel stood behind Marietta now, withered, rocking slightly, a husk of a man. He didn't look like any pillar to Ivy.

"Can we get a picture?" someone called out, and

Marietta said, "By all means, perhaps the steps of the courthouse would provide a pleasant setting...," and the whole group shuffled its way out into the bright sunshine. Ray and Ivy were positioned in front of Marietta and Lionel for a picture that would appear on the front page of the *Hammerhill Tribune* that very afternoon.

Their parents' lawyer had told Ray and Ivy what to do if a reporter asked to take their picture: say yes and look sad—"like you just lost your puppy." He said they had to play the sympathy card, since they didn't have a whole lot else going for them.

Ray had asked Ivy what the sympathy card was. Ivy didn't know, even though she and Dan played card games a lot. She wasn't bad at poker. "The wild card," she told him. "Kind of like the joker."

Now Ivy and Ray stood side by side, Marietta's veiny hand resting on Ivy's shoulder, Lionel's draped over Ray like a dead man's. Ivy was pretty sure that she and Ray looked, indeed, as if they had lost their puppy.

As they were posing for the picture, an impossibly long, shiny limousine pulled up in front of the courthouse, and a man in a uniform and cap stepped out and opened the side doors. Saying "Let us leave this sad business behind us" in her quavery voice, Marietta led Lionel and Ray and Ivy down the steps of the courthouse and toward the waiting vehicle.

Ivy hesitated before stepping into the dark opening; the car was so cavernous she felt she could be swallowed up by it. She looked back at the jagged steps of the courthouse, glinting in the sun, and at the knot of people standing there, watching Ray and her—and then, across the street, the last thing Ivy saw before she climbed into the limo: a little kid pedaling his red tricycle like mad, and a girl in flipflops trailing along, tapping the back of the bike with a stick, like she was the one who was making it go. Then Ray shoved Ivy from behind, and she climbed into the car and what felt like another world.

It smelled rich. Long leather seats that were more

like couches lined the sides, punctuated by wood-pan-eled tables with lots of buttons and knobs. There was even a little refrigerator with a gold handle, and a silver bowl set on top of it, filled with chocolate kisses!

"Is this where we're going to *live?*" Ray whispered once they had settled into their own cushy seat at the very back. He sounded hopeful.

"No!" Ivy said, even though she wasn't completely sure. It was clearly a car they were in—they'd begun moving, after all—but it was so beyond any car Ivy had ever been in before that it didn't seem possible that it was used *only* to get people from one place to another. She forced herself to concentrate. Her father

had taught her: *Always check a place out. Know your exits. Get the lay of the land.* Ivy studied the limousine. No bathroom, she realized. They couldn't live in a place that didn't have a bathroom. So she was right, and being right always lifted Ivy's spirits.

Seated opposite them, way down at the other end of the car—three blocks away, Ivy estimated—were Marietta and Lionel. Marietta stared straight ahead, past Ray and Ivy, as if they were invisible. Her gloved hands were folded on her lap. She looked pleased with herself, Ivy thought—because she had won, Ivy thought. Lionel was staring off, too, but at nothing, as if his eyes just rented space in his head and weren't connected

to his brain. Suddenly his chin dropped down against his chest and his eyes closed, and Ivy wondered, for a second, if he had died. But then she saw that his fingers were twitching and his eyeballs were moving around under his lids, and she realized that he had simply nodded off. Lionel's head bobbed in his sleep as they zoomed along, and Ivy turned her attention to the silver mound of chocolate kisses in the bowl.

Ray, meanwhile, had discovered the panel of buttons next to him and was trying them out one by one. He pressed the first silver button back, and the black screens covering the windows on either side lifted. Sunlight poured in and the outside world appeared before them. Downtown Hammerhill was gone, disappeared as if it had never been—no buildings, no jagged steps, no kids across the street. Now they were surrounded by open fields and rolling hills. The ride was smooth as a dream. Ivy leaned over to see more. It was beautiful out there, wherever they were.

They drove for a long time, or not that long—Ivy couldn't tell, it was all so smooth and dreamy; after a while, Ray fell asleep, too, his whole body leaning into hers. But Ivy fought the dreaminess. She didn't trust it and she kept her eyes wide open and studied Marietta, who seemed to be staring straight *through* Ivy, out into space, her mouth set in a tight, disagreeable smirk. How could she possibly be their match, Ivy wondered, remembering what her father had said. It seemed to her that Marietta was more like their *opposite*.

Eventually the car slowed a bit and then turned to the right between two enormous stone pillars—more pillars of society, Ivy figured. In the center of one, a gold plaque read La Grande Maison. Up the curving driveway they went, past rolling green lawns and huge, graceful trees—their budded-out limbs looked like they were dancing in the breeze, especially the weeping willows. Finally the limousine stopped beneath a portico supported by columns on either side. It was as if the entire driveway had been a long, winding extended tongue—a giraffe's, maybe—leading straight into an open mouth of enormous teeth.

Ivy craned to see, and Ray startled awake. He began to say something but got only as far as opening his mouth. Both he and Ivy stared out the window at the mansion before their eyes.

Marietta, meanwhile, down at the other end of the limousine, was trying to rouse Lionel. "We're home, dear," she said. "Lionel, darling..."

Suddenly the door opened—the chauffeur had come around and pulled it back—and more daylight flooded in; Ray and Ivy's screen expanded, and the house in front of them grew even bigger, bigger than any house they had seen except in movies. Ivy and Ray scrambled to get outside. Just before Ivy exited the limo, and with one quick swipe, she grabbed and pocketed nearly all the chocolate kisses.

"Veddy good," the driver said, and for an awful second Ivy thought she had been caught. She turned to him.

"What?" she said.

"Veddy good," he repeated.

What was he saying? Was he talking to them? (He was staring straight ahead.) Was he talking another language? Ivy suddenly got an idea: *they were in another country!*

"Where *are* we?" Ray said, still agog at the sight of the house.

"The Grand Mason," Ivy said. She had only the gold plaque to go by.

"Is *this* where we're going to live?" Ray asked again, as he had in the limo, and as unbelievable as it all seemed, Ivy said, "I bet it is."

Marietta and Lionel emerged with aching slowness from the limousine. The driver leaned down to grip Lionel's forearm and steady him on the pavement. Marietta whispered to the chauffeur, "You might have to *carry* him into the library," and for a startled second Ivy thought she had said *bury* him. "Then," Marietta instructed the driver, "bring their *things*," and with a wave of her wrist and flutter of fingers she motioned in the direction of Ray and Ivy.

She led the way up wide steps and across a broad porch. The front door was enormous and had, near its center, a giant gold knocker shaped like a fox's head. Just as Marietta reached the threshold, the door opened, pulled back by a sliver of a young woman dressed in a uniform clearly meant for a bigger maid. This one was lost inside her gray dress and white apron. She had stick-straight long hair the color of wheat pulled into two limp pigtails that hung over her tiny shoulders. She was slightly pigeon-toed. She looked, to Ivy, as though she had dressed up and was *playing* maid, except for her face, which was miserable and obviously not playing anything.

"They're here, Sissy," Marietta said to her in passing, as she swept into the entryway. "The *children*."

28

Sissy stared unabashedly at Ray and Ivy, as if she had never seen children before. But after just a few seconds her chin began to quiver and her gray eyes filled up with tears and Ivy thought she was going to burst our bawling right there in front of them.

Ivy abandoned her theory that they were in another country and wondered, instead, if they'd come to a place where everyone was crazy.

"Sissy," Marietta snapped, "*do* control yourself."

At the sound of Marietta's voice, Sissy jerked to attention, nodded her head, and dropped a twitchy curtsy, then lunged forward to close the door behind Ivy and Ray. Sissy's body seemed to be getting away from her, and Ivy stepped clear.

"That will be all," Marietta said, dismissing Sissy, and without another glance at Ray and Ivy she hurried off.

Marietta ushered them further into the entryway. It was the size of a movie theater.

"Be it ever so humble...," Marietta warbled, talking to the air.

Ivy was standing on a marble floor of alternating black and white stones in the shape of big diamonds, all arranged in a grand circle like a perfect and complete puzzle. She felt surrounded by space and more

29

space. Off to their left a sweeping staircase swirled up like some great promise to a whole other level of the house. The ceiling was so high up it seemed more of an indoor sky than a ceiling, and a huge chandelier hung down from it, suspended by a mighty gold chain. The room echoed as Marietta's heels clop, clop, clopped across to the staircase. Ivy and Ray followed behind, Ray stepping only on the white diamonds, Ivy only on the black.

Near the bottom of the stairs, against the wall, there was a fancy table with carved, curved, skinny legs—Ivy thought of manicured poodles with balls of fur at their ankles. Some kind of miniature building sat on top of the table, and in front of it, resting inside a wire holder, was a glass tube with silver caps on either end. Ivy thought it looked like something a king would read a proclamation from. A large glass dome covered the entire miniature building and the scroll, too. Ivy and Ray simultaneously stepped diagonally on their diamonds to get a closer look.

Marietta glanced over her shoulder and saw the children veering toward it. "Ah, the cake!" she said, turning—once again speaking to the air, as if some invisible audience had gathered in the entryway.

"Lionel's and my wedding cake," she announced.
"The work of Premier Bakers," she sniffed. "Of New
York City."

It *was* a cake—Ivy and Ray were studying it at eyeball

level, and there was no doubt that's what it was—but it was also a perfect replica of the house they were in, with all its pillars and porches and windows, complicated roofs and chimneys, layer upon layer of cake and frosting and curlicue.

Placed on the very top were two perfectly carved and dressed-up figures—a little bride and groom. Ivy especially liked the groom's tiny black silk top hat. It reminded her of her favorite Monopoly piece, the one she always chose when she and her father played, and for an instant she had an itch to somehow lift the glass dome that covered the cake and snatch the hat and put it in her pocket.

She leaned in closer. The cake was an amazing thing, but it was also creepy: so old and crusty that it seemed to Ivy more on the dead side of things, nothing anyone would ever want to eat. And there was a decrepit tilt to it, Ivy realized. The groom had sunk into frosting up to his left ankle so that one leg looked shorter than the other. The painted red lips of the bride—Marietta—had begun to bleed into the rest of her tiny carved face. Ivy and Ray made big eyes at each other through the glass dome.

Meanwhile, Marietta had warmed to her subject and

was still talking: about the wedding, and how grand it had been, a duke in attendance, the social event of the season...

Ray went back to gazing at the celestial ceiling, but Ivy couldn't seem to draw her eyes away from the preserved cake and its petrified flowers and roses and ribbons of hardened frosting. She studied the silver-capped glass cylinder. There was a piece of thick paper rolled up inside the tube, and a few fancy letters were visible, written in gold.

But then Ivy saw something else entirely: out of the back corner of the cake crept a crumb-laden spider, about the size of a quarter, dark and thick, like moving moss. It inched forward, closer to the edge of the glass dome, then stopped, turned, and crept back into the foundation of the big cake house.

Ivy stood frozen in place. What she had seen! Only now it was gone, disappeared, as if, perhaps, it had never been. She didn't know which was worse—seeing it, or not seeing it but knowing it was there, inside— and she felt a little sick. But she was glad Ray hadn't seen it. Ray was scared of spiders.

"Come along, then," Marietta said suddenly. She had reached the end of her recitation—something about the world-famous calligrapher who had lettered their wedding certificate—and was headed upstairs.

With a start, Ivy hurried to follow her, racing across both black and white diamonds, anxious to be as far away from the spider in the cake as she could get.

She took Ray's hand and they followed along together, behind Marietta, mounting the spiraling, most richly carpeted steps their feet had ever set foot on. Highly polished gold dowels with knobs at either end held the carpet flat against the back of each riser. Ivy thought the staircase was like the limousine: way too fancy for simply getting people from one place to another. She suspected more mysterious uses.

At the top of the stairs, the hallway extended for what Ivy estimated to be several miles in either direction. Life-size, gold-framed portraits hung along the walls as far as Ivy could see. None of the people in them—all men—were smiling.

Turning to face Ray and Ivy, and sweeping her arm to the left, Marietta announced, "Lionel and I occupy the West Wing of the house. We've feathered *your* nests in the East Wing"—and she extended her other arm to the right—"where I *trust* you will be comfortable during your stay, and where I fully expect you to stay *put*."

Marietta had a fancy way of talking, but Ivy knew they were being given orders, and she hated being bossed. Some of what Marietta was saying, though— about nests, and wings, and feathers—sounded good

to Ivy. Maybe birds lived upstairs, in the East and West Wings. She remembered the giant atrium at the zoo she and Ray had gone to with Carol and Dan. The birds lived in a place so big and open she hadn't even known it was a cage until her father pointed it out.

Marietta was leading the way down the hall. She identified each portrait she passed as some famous person in her family. *Bragger*, Ivy thought. Marietta wasn't the only one with famous people in her family. Their grampa was famous. Their Grampa Blackie had pulled off one of the biggest bank robberies in the state of California.

On and on they went, down the dim hallway. Ray and Ivy padded along behind Marietta, and the thick carpet swallowed up every sound but the jingle-jangle of her bracelet. "Here," Marietta said finally, stopping at a door to her left. "Your room and bath," and she extended her hand, inviting them both to step in.

Again, as in the entryway, it was space that greeted Ivy—space that struck and surrounded her. Another big room, mostly air, with a four-poster double bed, its wooden posts pointing straight up, topped with what looked like carved pineapples. The bed sat high up off the floor, and Ivy thought of "The Princess and the Pea," of course, although it really wasn't *that* high, covered with a white bedspread with satiny curlicues embroidered all across it. There was a fancy cabinet built into the corner of the room, loaded from top to bottom with dolls in costumes, all protected by a bowed glass door with a key in its lock. Ivy stepped closer to see. She was interested in the key, not the dolls; she'd never had much use for dolls.

"Ah, yes," Marietta sniffed. "My collection. From around the world."

It was a skeleton key—Ivy knew from Dan that that was the name for it—resting within the bright brass lock. A tall dresser with gold handles stood against the other wall, and a desk and chair, everything as neat and polished as the courtroom had been. There were

no birds. The windows, two of them, stretched as tall as three of her and had sills deep enough to sit on. They looked out over the portico and down the rolling lawn of the estate. The drapes, heavy and quiet, were drawn to the side, and the filmy liner behind them softened the sunlight that streamed into the room.

"And your bath," Marietta continued, turning the glass knob of a door Ivy had thought was a closet. But it opened into the most sparkling bathroom Ivy had ever seen. Things glistened: the full-length mirror, the faucets in the sink and the deep claw-foot tub—deep enough, Ivy thought, to do a complete underwater flip in. Tiny bright white tiles covered the walls and the floor. Fat folded towels hung everywhere. Like a hotel! Ivy thought. They had stayed in a few, Carol and Dan and Ray and her. The Ritz, once, and they had had room service.

Marietta crossed through the bathroom, her heels clicking loudly on the tiles, to yet another door that led to yet another bedroom. "And this will be yours, young man," she said to Ray.

Ivy and Ray looked back into Ivy's room, then through the bathroom and into Ray's. The beauty, the *perfection* of the layout washed over them: side-by-side rooms connected by one in the middle, a secret passageway, just for them. Ivy started a list in her head of what to include in the map they would draw of the big house: a wing of their own, all the exits, a tub like a swimming pool...

"Well?" Marietta said. "What say you? Will it *do*?"

In all the places Ray and Ivy had lived—and they had lived in plenty; their father called himself a traveling man and had taught Carol, Ray, and Ivy how to travel fast and light—they had never been asked if any place they'd been brought to would *do*. Ivy and Ray turned to Marietta without an answer.

Finally Ray said, "Do what?"

And Marietta laughed at him!—not a pretty laugh; it sounded gravel-filled and ended abruptly, as if it had been a bad idea. "Next time, perhaps you'll know enough to say, 'It will do quite nicely,'" she told him. And then she said, "Lionel and I nap in the afternoon. And given what a busy day it's been, we'll dine in our quarters tonight. Sissy will prepare a supper for you in the kitchen. Is that everything?" she wondered, to the air. "Food, accommodations...what more could children possibly need?" She focused on Ray and Ivy once again. "Nothing," she said, answering her own question. "So I leave you to your own devices," she told them, and she did.

Their Own Devices

"We start here," Ivy said, pointing to the tub.

Ray nodded.

"Then through my room," Ivy continued.

"I could go through mine," Ray said. "And you go through yours. And we could meet."

"Right," Ivy said. "That's what I meant. We'll cross in the hall, then run backwards past old Mustache Man"—she meant the portrait that was hanging between Ray's room and hers. "She thinks her family is so great," Ivy said.

"Whole way running?" Ray asked.

Ivy considered. Hopping? "Skipping," she said. She was a tremendously fast skipper. "Skipping in the hallway, running everywhere else. Back through each other's room, first person both legs in the tub wins."

"OK," Ray agreed, and they both leaned over to take off their shoes. They always raced barefoot.

They climbed into the tub. The enamel felt smooth against the bottoms of her feet. The tub was even deeper than Ivy had estimated. It could hold, she calculated, enough water to fill an entire waterbed. Dan and Carol had had a waterbed once, in one of the places they lived.

They each drew in their breath. "On your maaark, get set..." Ray and Ivy had called so many races in unison that their voices together made one. "*Go!*" they popped.

It took Ray longer to scramble out of the tub and make the cut to his room. Ivy was already zipping by her four-poster, heading for the door. She was just crossing the threshold into the hallway, stretching into the first lunge of skipping, when she plowed into the driver, who had appeared with their bags—Ivy's ratty little suitcase in his left hand and Ray's ratty little suitcase in his right. He dropped both bags as he doubled over, and was eye to eye with Ivy when he said, "I'd watch my step if I were you..."

Even though Ivy understood his words, she didn't know what he was telling her.

Ray emerged just then from his bedroom door, stopping himself mid-skip. Ivy took a giant step back from the driver. He had straightened up and reclaimed himself, but his cap had shifted awkwardly in their collision.

"Time out!" Ivy called to Ray, to halt the race—which killed her to do, because she had been ahead.

"Where shall I put these?" the driver asked, speaking formally once again.

"That's my room," she told him, pointing.

"And this is mine," Ray called out, pointing to his.

"Veddy well, then," he said, and stepping around Ivy, entered her room. He snapped open a special contraption with polished wooden legs and straps of material crisscrossed on top that clearly had been made simply to hold a suitcase. Until she saw its use Ivy had thought it was just broken furniture. Then the driver came back out into the hall—he had straightened his cap—and walked down to Ray's room. Ivy was relieved he didn't go through their connecting bathroom. She wanted the passageway to be just for Ray and her.

The driver came out of Ray's room empty-handed, and asked, "Will there be anything else?"

Ivy didn't know. Would there be? "Probably," she said.

"I beg your pardon?"

"This will do quite nicely," Ray piped up. That's what Marietta had been looking for—*This will do quite nicely*—and Ivy was sorry she hadn't thought to say it first.

Once again the driver said, "Veddy well, then," and

turned and started down the hallway. But he went in the opposite direction from the grand staircase and disappeared to the right at the very end of the hall. Another exit, Ivy noted.

"Come on," she said to Ray, and led the way back to her room.

Ray asked if she wanted to race again, but Ivy said no. Her collision with Veddy—that's what she was already calling the driver—had shaken her up a bit. In her bedroom, she looked out her window over the rolling lawn of the estate. Suddenly it seemed endless to her, waving goodbye smack into the horizon. She went and sat down next to Ray on her bed.

The parts of the day that hadn't been so good were pushing up inside her thinking; sometimes that happened late in the afternoon, sometimes when she couldn't get to sleep at night. Now she was remembering the spider in the cake, and crybaby Sissy, and Marietta's unblinking face in the limousine, and then suddenly, *bam*, the judge! Guilty! Twenty-five years! Oh, her parents' black and red curls! It came as a shock all over again, and she sat straight up as if she had been pinched.

"What?" Ray said.

She shook her head. "We gotta face the music," she said. They were words right out of her father's mouth, and it felt comforting, somehow, to say them.

Ray looked at her for more.

"This stinks," she continued. She didn't know exactly what it was that stank, but she was convinced that something did. "We need a plan," she told Ray.

He watched her, waiting.

The idea of making a plan buoyed Ivy. She was good at plans. And it wasn't like they hadn't been in tough spots before. There had been other dirty deals, other times her parents had been left holding the bag, other times that one or the other of them had spent time in jail.

"Yeah," Ray agreed.

Ivy loved how Ray always jumped on board with her. Now he was sitting up straighter, too.

"We have to check the place out. Get the lay of the land," Ivy said.

"Let's go," Ray answered.

She and Ray tiptoed down to the far end of the hall, to track the route Veddy had taken. More big, dark portraits lined the walls—serious men in gold frames whose eyes seemed to watch their every move. But the last picture, at the very end, by the landing to what they saw was a back staircase, was covered. A black sheet had been fitted over the four corners of the frame as if it were a mattress. Ray and Ivy stopped and stared at it. It gave Ivy the creeps, even more than the uncovered portraits. She and Ray turned and asked each other with wide eyes what they were looking at.

"Maybe the painting didn't turn out very good," Ray suggested.

"Then why would they hang it?" Ivy said. "And *none* of them are good," she pointed out.

They stared at it in silence again.

"Maybe the person died," Ray said.

"I bet they're *all* dead," Ivy answered, gesturing back to the other pictures lining the wall.

"Then why's it covered?" Ray asked.

What was worse than dead? Ivy didn't know, and she was torn: she wanted to lift up the sheet and peek. But she was a little scared, too. She remembered the spider in the cake. "C'mon," she told Ray, and headed downstairs. They could investigate the covered painting later.

The narrow wooden steps were so different from the carpeted spiral of the grand stairway. "This one must be for the servants," Ivy said. She knew from old movies that servants lived underneath the rich people they worked for, and had to use different stairs. These steps landed Ray and Ivy in the kitchen.

Sissy was standing at the sink scraping carrots, and the instant she saw them her face crumpled and she turned away, back to her carrots, peeling like mad. Ivy watched as her narrow little shoulders began to twitch, as if every little thing in the world set her off.

Ivy and Ray looked at each other and grimaced. Then they bolted for the back door and let it bang shut behind them as they tore around to the front of the house

and across the driveway. There, with the big house solidly behind them and the velvety grass cool and smooth beneath their bare feet, they stood still for a moment, looking out over the great expanse of rolling lawn. Ivy had a sudden thought of the ocean, the water shifting the sand and planting her up to her ankles. She and Ray and Carol and Dan had spent part of one summer at the ocean, and now her feet were remembering.

Then, just as suddenly as they had stopped, they were off—both of them, running, up and down the hills, heading straight toward the maze of gardens as if they knew exactly where they were going and what they were going to do next. Ivy had a feeling that the farther they got from the big house, the better off they'd be, and she was in front, leading the charge, when she heard Ray call out, "Wait." They had just rounded a huge stand of rhododendron bushes.

As soon as Ivy turned back she saw what had caught Ray's attention: a gap in the lower branches of the biggest bush that looked like a tunnel entrance. They instantly dropped to their knees and crawled inside. They were both panting and proceeding along on all fours, and they began barking to each other and barked their way into the center of the bush, where the roots rose up out of the ground and turned into the branches that arched over them now like a leafy umbrella. The underside they had discovered was dim and cool and perfectly private; there was just the right amount of room for them to sit close together, cross-legged in the middle of it.

"Good surveillance," Ivy said when she caught her breath, just the way her father did whenever one of them spotted something worth checking out. She thought they had lucked out to find a place for themselves so soon.

"Was she *crying*?" Ray wanted to know.

"Who?" Ivy looked at her brother's questioning face, and then she remembered Sissy's skinny back shaking inside her gray uniform. "Yeah," she said. "We've definitely got a crier on our hands." She nodded at Ray. "Some people just do," she told him. "Cry."

"Oh," Ray said. Their family didn't, much.

"Even her name," Ivy continued. "Think about it— they didn't name her Sissy for nothing."

Ray solemnly took in what Ivy was telling him.

"So we should elect officers," Ivy said. It's what they always did when they found a new hideout.

Ivy liked being President and Secretary. There was nothing about President she didn't like—she even liked the *sound* of it—and she loved Secretary practically as much as President because she liked to write.

Ray was always Vice-President and Treasurer. Their father said that he who controls the money controls the world, which made Ray feel good about being Treasurer, even though what he mostly kept track of were the votes in their elections, and whatever puny dues they managed to scrape together.

But Ivy and Ray held an election at each new place they settled in, to be fair.

Since they didn't have any paper or pencils they turned back to back and voted in the dirt, using a twig to make their marks.

Then Ray, the newly elected Vice-President, announced

the results—Ivy, President and Secretary; Ray, Vice-President and Treasurer—and Ivy, in her capacity as Secretary, marked the results in the dirt with her stick. When she was done she wished more than ever that she had a hammer to thwack against something and make the sound that started and ended everything. But thinking of the hammer reminded her again of the judge, and the trial, and the crummy verdict, and she announced, "We need evidence."

"For what?" Ray said.

"Against Marietta. This is all her fault," Ivy said. It felt so good to say it that she knew she had to be right.

"*What* evidence?" Ray wanted to know. They didn't usually look for evidence. Usually they settled on dues—how much they each had to pay to be in the club—and what they would get with their money. Or they drew a map of wherever they were. Their father had taught them how useful a floor plan could be.

Ivy almost said, "I don't know," but she caught herself. She was remembering the evidence from her parents' trial—receipts and letters and signed documents. They didn't have any of those, and she didn't know where to get them. Or even what crime to charge

Marietta with. "It takes time to collect stuff," she said. "Exhibit A and B and C."

"OK," Ray agreed. "But let's get food, too," he added. They always kept food in their hideouts.

"Hey!" Ivy remembered, and she emptied out the stash of chocolate kisses from her pocket.

She and Ray each grabbed one and peeled off its silver foil. They combined their wrappings and started a silver ball with them. The chocolate was soft and gooey and coated the roof of Ivy's mouth.

"We could charge her with kidnapping," she said after a while.

"Her who?" Ray said, reaching for another kiss.

Ivy clicked her tongue in disgust. "Marietta," she said. "Who *else*? I mean, we didn't ask to stay with her and Lionel. They just kind of took us."

"Yeah," Ray said, "but in a limo..."

"So what?" Ivy said. "You think you can't get kidnapped in a limo?"

Ray shrugged. "Didn't the judge tell her to?"

"Oh, what does *he* know?" Ivy snapped. But Ray had a point. They'd probably have a hard time making the kidnapping charge stick. Especially if they got the same judge for a trial. How many judges were there in Hammerhill anyway? Did they all have mustaches? There had to be *something* they could charge Marietta with, Ivy thought. She helped herself to another kiss and added the tin foil to their pea-sized ball.

Ivy and Ray ate all the chocolates she had swiped from the limo, but Ivy didn't come up with any definite charge against Marietta. "We will, though," she promised. "Even if it takes twenty-five years!"

A while later, as Ray and Ivy lingered, full and quiet, in their hideout, the branches of the bush suddenly quivered, and they heard someone or something pass by outside. Ivy drew her finger up to her lips, and she and Ray froze. After a few seconds they peeked outside and saw Veddy making his way up the hill.

"What's *he* doing here?" Ivy said. Was he following them? "Let's follow *him*," she said, and Ray, who was excellent at sneaking up on people, instantly agreed.

They crept all the way out from the bush and proceeded to trail behind him, still partially crouched down, the way they did when they did their sneaking. They followed him to a fork in the driveway that led into a wooded section of the estate, and ended at a neat brick house with little flower boxes outside the windows and a welcome mat at the front door. Once Veddy had disappeared inside, Ray and Ivy made a slow, crouched approach to the window and stretched to their tiptoes to take a peek. There, instead of the living room Ivy expected to see—with a TV, and maybe Veddy plunked down in a chair in front of it—they found the limo!

"It's the *garage*?" she said, incredulous that someone would make so fancy a place just to hold a car. The back of the building had a full-size garage door, and there was a staircase off to the side.

"Let's sneak in," Ray begged.

But Ivy didn't want to. Just knowing what it was and that it was there was enough for her; besides, she had already emptied the candy dish.

Suddenly, behind them, out of nowhere, stood Veddy.

"Keeping an eye on one another, are we?" he asked.

Ivy froze; she couldn't think of what to say.

"Do you get to *live* with the car?" Ray asked.

Veddy considered Ray. "I beg your pardon?"

"Do you—" Ray started again, but then Veddy answered.

"I maintain my quarters here, yes," he said.

"Nice place," Ivy said, reaching for Ray's hand. "It will do quite nicely," she said, even as she began to pull Ray away, back where they'd come from. "See you around," she said.

Veddy watched them, wearing an odd expression. It might have been a smile. Or not. "Indubitably," he said.

Back in their hideout, Ray was still talking about the limo.

"Maybe he'd let us sit in it," Ray said. Ray and Ivy spent a lot of time playing in Dan's car, driving each other to Las Vegas or Miami Beach or New York City.

"Maybe," Ivy said. But she didn't think so, didn't really want to. She wasn't sure about Veddy.

"We could ask," Ray said.

"Forget about Veddy," Ivy told him. "He's only the driver. We have bigger fish to fry. More important things to do."

"We do?"

"Ray!" Ivy said, exasperated. Sometimes she could hardly believe how much more she knew than he did. "Surveillance," she reminded him. "Case the joint! Get Marietta!" she finished.

"C'mon," she said, and led him out of their hideout. There was more of the estate to size up. "Look." She directed Ray's attention to the garden spread out before them—like its own little city, with paths and crossroads that ran in between the meticulously laid-out raised flower beds. And she was especially glad to be able to say, "They have a pergola," because she loved that word and knew what it meant, and she sounded, at least to herself, very grown-up saying it. When Ray didn't bother to ask her what a pergola was, she continued anyway, as if he had.

"This thing," she said, leading him over to the wooden structure. Vines and flowers climbed up

its slats and wrapped around the boards on top and dripped all around Ivy.

"It has an open roof," she said, just as her father had. She was remembering perfectly her seventh birthday. Dan had taken her to the teahouse at the Huntington Gardens in the City of Angels to celebrate. When they got there, the woman at the door tried to turn them away because they didn't have a reservation. But her father had put both his hands on Ivy's shoulders and said, "Meet my daughter, Ivy. Today is Ivy's seventh birthday. Do you honestly think I would fail to make a reservation for my one and only daughter on her one and only seventh birthday? What do you *take* me for?" The woman's face had turned red and kind of melted and she said how terribly sorry she was, but Dan Fitts was very nice to her and told her not to feel bad, that it wasn't her fault—she hadn't been the person he'd spoken to, obviously—and that the table for two, in the corner, by the window, would be perfect, no harm done, and she led them over to it. Then Ivy and her father ate all the strawberries and little sandwiches and bite-sized desserts they wanted, and sometime in between all their eating her father had pointed out the pergola in the garden and given her the word for it. She had not forgotten one bit of that day.

Ray wanted to race through the garden right away. They did a short running/hopping combo around the roses. Ivy won and Ray called for two out of three, but Ivy wouldn't. She said there was still more land to get the lay of. "We can race again tomorrow," she told him. "Or at sundown." She always liked that word: *sundown*. "Or at *midnight*," she said, warming to the sound of her own ideas. Midnight was even better than sundown.

"Yeah," Ray said, right on board.

"We could run a midnight race," Ivy sang out, "in the moonlight!"

It was such an obviously good idea that they promised each other then and there that they would do it: run a garden race, at midnight, in the moonlight. They brought their foreheads together to seal the deal.

"At the next full moon," Ivy declared, and she liked the sound of that best of all.

They explored the entire estate. Ray got thirsty and they both got tired, but Ivy said they had to be tough. "We're traversing the land," she informed Ray: that wonderful word, *traversing*, arriving in her mind like a special-delivery gift. She was thinking of all the Westerns she had watched on TV, with Dan. She was remembering one in particular, where the rancher's horse got a broken leg and the rancher had to walk and walk and walk, parched and baking in the sun, but he kept going.

She and Ray were making their way up a slow-rising hill, above and beyond the gardens. At the crest, Ivy drew in her breath at what they found stretched out down below: the river—for as far as she could see. The water came as a complete surprise.

"This is definitely a good sign," she told Ray.
"It is?"

"Yep," she said, and opened her arms to the scene before them. "That's where Dan and Carol are," she told him. "Up the river."

They stood and looked hard at it, following its trail for as long and far as they could.

"Where?" Ray finally said, craning.

"You can't actually see from here," she told him. "But they're there."

On the Inside

When they finally returned to the big house, no one was waiting for them. The whole place seemed deserted. Even crybaby Sissy was gone. On the table in the kitchen, there were two settings, and two plates covered with tin foil. Ivy and Ray pulled out their chairs and sat down and uncovered their meals. They flattened and folded the foil to add to their silver ball the next day.

"Where do you think *Sissy* lives?" Ray asked.

"Maybe in a broom closet that's built like a little house," Ivy said. "Or maybe she lives with Veddy and the limo. Veddy and Sissy," she said, trying out their names together. But the combo didn't sound right to her, nothing like Dan and Carol.

"Maybe she just lives with her family somewhere," Ray said. "In a regular place."

"Maybe," Ivy said with a shrug.

Dinner was a tuna fish sandwich and chips and carrot and celery sticks, and that was fine by them except for the carrot and celery sticks. Sitting in the kitchen and eating her dinner with Ray felt all right to Ivy. The kitchen was the one room in the big house that seemed normal to her. Just the sound of the refrigerator humming, and the feel of the sandwich in her hands, and the sight of the toaster on the counter— they were things Ivy was used to—and, of course, sitting across from Ray and seeing his face.

"Do Dan and Carol get to eat together?" Ray asked. He was building a fort with his celery and carrot sticks.

Ivy didn't think they did, but she didn't want to say so. "Definitely on Christmas," she told him. "And their birthdays. And anniversary."

"With lobster," Ray agreed. That's what Dan and Carol always had on special occasions.

"And champagne," Ivy said.

When they had eaten as much of their sandwiches as they were going to, Ivy suggested that they explore some more, and they left the kitchen through the swinging door with the diamond of glass in it, too high up for Ivy or Ray to look through. That door opened into an enormous room with a table long enough to seat twenty, and fancy upholstered chairs and heavy brocade drapes and candelabras.

"*Another* dining room?" Ray said. But this one was like in a castle. Ivy imagined herself dressed in a robe—like the judge wore, but longer, and with a train, one that needed to be carried—and she led Ray in a procession around the table, tapping the back of each chair as if with a wand. There was a portrait hanging at the far end of the room: Marietta sitting up straight on a white couch, wearing her horrible smile.

"They should put a sheet on *that* one," Ray said, staring, and Ivy agreed.

They went from the dining room into the grand entry hall. They made up a game where they had to take thirteen steps—not more, not less—on either the black or the white tiles to get to the staircase. Every time Ivy hopped by the cake, she admired the silk top hat on the carved groom and the fancy scroll on its holder, and she made herself not think about the spider.

"Hey," Ray called to her. He had gone into one of

the other rooms off the entryway. Ivy had just taken her twelfth step, but she left her diamond and went to find him. The room she peered into was filled with books, floor to ceiling on every wall. She had never seen so many books outside a public library, and stepping inside, she liked how it felt being surrounded by them. She started reading aloud some of the titles, stamped in gold on fancy leather bindings: *Paradise Lost, Crime and Punishment, War and Peace...*

But Ray hadn't called her in to look at books. He wanted to show her the chair he was sitting in. "Watch," he said, and he pressed a button at the end of a cord. Slowly the chair began to spread out: a section beneath his feet rose, and the back tilted down toward the floor. When he pressed another button it folded up again and

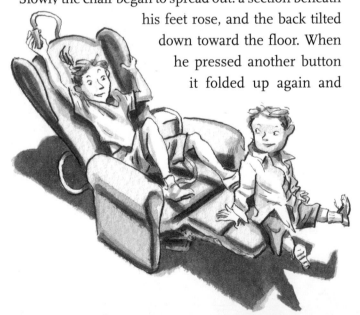

raised and tilted forward to deliver him to a standing position.

"Lemme try," Ivy said, and she made the chair do all it could do. It reminded her of a hospital bed they had visited someone in, once. "*Good* chair," she declared.

Ray didn't answer. He was looking at the newspaper lying on the big desk in the center of the room, and he was looking at *them*—Ray and Ivy and Lionel and Marietta—staring out from its front page. "Hey, it's *us*!" he said.

Ivy hopped out of the chair to see for herself.

"What's it say?" he asked.

Ivy read the headline: *Nolands Rescue Lost Children.*

"Lost!" Ray said. "We're right here."

"Oh, *they* don't know," Ivy said, tossing it back down on the desk. "You can't believe what you read," she told him. "Especially in a newspaper. They just put any words that fit." Still, she felt a little sick. The picture was as wrong as it could be. They hadn't been *rescued*! And it should have been Dan and Carol in the picture, curls and Dan's big smile, like the photo of their family on Ray's fifth birthday, when they'd all gone to the racetrack.

On second thought she snatched up the paper

again. She tore out the picture and put it in her pocket. "It can be our first piece of evidence," she said proudly. "It's a lie."

The picture reminded Ivy of the need for continued surveillance. She called off their diamond-hopping game and ordered an inspection of the other rooms adjoining the entryway. They checked out a little bath-room that had gold faucet handles and smelled like someone had spilled perfume in it. They made faces and closed the door when they got a whiff.

The living room reminded Ivy of a museum she had gone to once, on a class trip. There was a big mirror in a heavy gold frame and fancy chairs that looked related to thrones and little stools set in front of them, for resting your feet on. One was embroidered with needlepoint and said *Where there's a will there's a way*. The main thing in the room, though, was the portrait of an old man hanging over the fireplace. He was seated in one of the thronelike chairs, staring straight out, looking furious.

"That must be old Moneybags," Ivy said. "The 'dear departed father,'" she said, and she made her voice all quavery, like Marietta's.

Ray and Ivy stared up at him for a while. "Who'd

want to sit here with him breathing down your neck?"
Ivy said. "No one," she said, answering her own question. And in fact, the living room didn't look as if anyone ever actually sat in it.

Ray and Ivy went back to the entryway. They hadn't gathered additional evidence, but Ivy said knowing the floor plan counted.

"So can we race now?" Ray asked.

"OK," Ivy said, "but upstairs."

They went to their rooms and put on their pj's and settled on a running-forwards-and-backwards race up and down the long hall, from the covered portrait to the top of the grand staircase and back again. On the second run they dared each other to pluck the corner of the sheet that covered the painting, enough to make the whole thing ripple like a black wave. Meanwhile everything down in the West Wing stayed dark and quiet and sealed up like a tomb.

They raced for a while—best of three, and then three out of five, and then their final winner-take-all extravaganza. It grew late, but no one told them to call it a day or knock off the racket. They finally just got so tired on their own that they made their way into Ray's room, and Ray climbed into bed, ready for a story.

Ivy did her best to sound like Dan. "This is the story of Rindercella and her wicked mepstother and three sigly usters," she began. She couldn't tell it exactly the way Dan did, but Ray still laughed at the *pransome hince* and the *moke of stridnight* and of course when *Rindercella slopped her dripper.* "They lel in fuv," Ivy finished, "and lived heverly ever hapwards."

Ray chuckled into his pillow and Ivy knew it was OK for her to go.

She walked through the glistening bathroom to her own room, pleased to have ended their day on a good note. She was looking forward to climbing up onto her high mattress and lifting back the covers, the way she imagined a princess might put herself to bed after a long, hard day. No one hollered at her to turn off the bathroom light, so she just left it on.

Finally Ivy relaxed into her deep and comfy mattress. The pillows were soft. Maybe the big house wasn't going to be so bad after all. If Marietta left them alone. Plus they had their hideout in the rhododendron bush. And the race to run, in the moonlight, at the moke of stridnight. And they had their ball of silver, and their first piece of evidence. Maybe she could find a hammer— oh, what she could do with a hammer...! Her fingers

closed into a soft, sleepy fist and then released. In no time at all Ivy was dreaming.

The big house was quiet, and Ray and Ivy slept soundly through their first night inside it.

There was only one problem: Ray wet his bed.

Practice

Ray and Ivy knew exactly what to do when Ray wet the bed, because it happened a fair amount—whenever they made a quick switch to a new place, or anytime they had to start school. Ray told Ivy, "The rain in Spain falls mainly on the plain"—which is how their father always put it—and then Ivy helped Ray strip the sheets off his bed and roll them up and toss them in the corner or stuff them in the bathtub until the next time anyone went to the laundromat. It was never a big deal.

Until they landed at the big house.

That morning Sissy came upstairs and told them, "Breakfast in ten minutes. Mrs. Noland is expecting you." She wouldn't look at Ray or Ivy, just stared down at the floor like a shy girl in a hurry to say what she had to say and be gone. As she was leaving, though, she saw the wadded-up sheets on Ray's floor, and she gasped. "What happened?" she said, as if something terrible had. "Oh, Mrs. Noland won't like this one *tiny* bit," she said, distraught.

Ray held still and Ivy stepped forward to explain about the rain in Spain. She hadn't even finished, though, when Sissy scooted across and gathered the sheets. Her about-to-bawl look was all over her. "*Please* don't go making trouble," she begged as she scurried out the door.

Ivy didn't like the way things were going. "C'mon, Ray," she said, "let's make up the bed anyway."

"What?" Ray asked her. "Are we in trouble?"

"What's a little rain?" she answered him. "But we'll make up the bed just in case." And she got him to help her stretch the bedspread as wrinkle-free as they could over the mattress, and put the pillows in place. "There," she said, and she felt better. The bed looked fine to her, covered up like nothing at all had happened.

Then they went downstairs for breakfast. They crossed the entryway, tiptoed past the glass-domed cake, and peeked into the dining room. Marietta was already seated at one end of the table. Lionel sat at the far other end, as far away as he had been in the limousine, hunched over and reading the newspaper with a magnifying glass. Places had been set for Ray and Ivy on either side of Marietta, and she motioned for them to come and sit down.

The heavy brocade drapes were pulled against the morning sunshine. Approaching Marietta, Ivy could feel something was wrong, even more wrong than it always was around Marietta. She and Ray advanced, as they'd been told to, but reluctantly. They silently took their places, slipping onto the upholstered seats. Ivy's feet didn't begin to reach the floor, and she concentrated on not swinging them. She knew they were in trouble—the air felt wavy with it.

"I trust you slept well," Marietta began. She held a glass of prune juice midway to her mouth. "And that you are ready for your breakfast," she said, and no sooner were the words out of her mouth than Sissy appeared through the swinging door, carrying a tray loaded with food. Ivy noted with relief that she wasn't crying. Serving Marietta first, she set down a small, circular contraption with handles, and beside it, a boiled egg in a glazed cup shaped like an 8. The dish looked as if it had been specially made just to hold the egg; Ivy thought of the suitcase stand upstairs in her bedroom, specially made to hold a suitcase, and the garage-like-a-house, just for the limo.

Then Sissy came and stood by Ivy, holding out the tray and its contents—a big silver bowl filled with cereal, another overflowing with strawberries, and a painted plate piled high with strips of bacon and fancy tongs for picking them up.

The sight of all that food made Ivy momentarily forget that there was trouble in the air. She helped herself to the bacon. She took plenty. Ray heaped strawberries onto his plate, and he and Ivy jiggled their eyebrows at each other across the table. Nothing about Marietta encouraged them to make sounds of any sort, even words.

Once Sissy had disappeared back into the kitchen, Marietta took a small sip of her juice, placed her glass back on the table, and announced, "I hear there was a mishap in the night."

Ivy wondered what a mishap was as she crunched her bacon. She liked bacon, and she liked it cooked just the way it was: well-done.

"An unfortunate *accident*," Marietta reiterated.

Ivy knew what an accident was, and so did Ray, and they instantly stopped chewing.

Marietta's voice dropped lower and had no quaver in it at all when she said, "One that I trust will *not* happen again."

Ray and Ivy looked at each other across the table.

"Because if it *were* to happen again," she went on, "something would have to be *done*." Marietta picked up the circular contraption in front of her and positioned it over the top of the egg. She pinched the handles together and a circle of little teeth emerged and sank into the eggshell. With one quick motion Marietta lifted off the decapitated top of her egg.

Ivy and Ray watched the whole process, spellbound.

"*Be* no trouble," Marietta said as she set the egg trimmer aside and carefully spooned the first bite of egg out of its shell, "and there *will be* no trouble." She raised her head and looked first at Ivy, then at Ray. "Have I made myself clear?"

Clear as mud: that's what her father often said, and

Ivy could hear him saying it now, inside her head, but she knew better than to say it out loud, just as she had known better than to swing her legs. She studied her brother's scared face and his ears, red with shame. "May we be excused?" she said. She remembered someone saying that in an old-fashioned movie she had seen.

Marietta turned to Ivy, eyebrows arched. "Already?" she said, but clearly she was open to the idea of them disappearing. "Fine, then," she said. "Go. Go outside." She danced her fingers out at them, shooing them away. "*Play*," she said—another word that sounded dirty when she said it.

Ray and Ivy looked like they were practicing for a fire drill at school—forcing themselves to walk, not run—as they filed past Marietta and left the dining room. They cut through the kitchen and exited out the back door. As soon as they stepped outside they practically burst out of their skin running—straight to their hideout in the rhododendron bush. But just before Ivy crawled inside she turned back and saw Ray's sheets, hung out to dry on the clothesline, billowing and blowing for all the world to see. Like flags, like banners. Like war, she thought.

"Sissy," she hissed as she made her way into the hideout and settled herself next to Ray. "She ratted us out."

"She did?" Ray said.

"Who else?" Ivy said. "She told about the rain in Spain. She must have."

Ray only looked miserable, and Ivy couldn't stand to see it.

"Don't worry about it," she told him. "We'll get her. Sissy *and* Marietta. We'll get them all." And then she remembered: "We have evidence!" She reached into her back pocket to produce the newspaper picture. The tin foil she had flattened from dinner the night before also fell out, and the sight of both things cheered her. "Bring yours?" she asked Ray.

He produced the foil from his pocket, and they each added theirs to the silver ball. Then Ivy officially called the meeting to order. She made the gathering of more evidence the first item on the agenda.

Ray wasn't so sure. "What *is* it?" he wanted to know. "Evidence."

"It *proves* stuff," she told him.

"Like what?" he said.

"Whatever you want it to," she said, exasperated. Hadn't he paid a bit of attention at Dan and Carol's trial?

"But what *fun* is it?" he said.

"It's important, Ray," she countered. "Enough evidence and you can send someone to jail and throw away the key." She flung her arm out in dramatic enactment and whacked the lowest branch of the bush.

Ray sighed. "What's *that* prove?" he said, pointing to the picture from the newspaper.

Ivy looked down at it. "It proves they're wrong," she said. "About us. And it proves they're liars."

"You can go to jail for lying?" Ray asked, alarmed.

Ivy considered. "If it's a huge lie," she said, fairly

sure. "A real whopper. And if you're a grown-up," she added quickly. "Kids don't go to jail for lying. Kids don't go to jail, period." She deeply hoped everything she was saying was true.

"So could we really get Marietta thrown in jail?" he asked.

"If we play our cards right," Ivy told him. "We should practice, though. Let's hold a trial. I'll be the judge." She sat up a little straighter. "And the jury," she added. She didn't mean to hog, but she felt about being judge and jury the way she did about being President and Secretary: quite sure.

"Who am I?" Ray wanted to know.

Ivy considered what other parts were left. "Wanna be the guy who calls out 'All rise' when the judge comes in?"

Ray shrugged. "OK," he said.

"You can say it like Veddy," she told him, and they practiced for a while, until Ray was practically hollering "*All rrrrise*," rolling out the sound like he was some kind of opera singer.

"But we need a robe," Ivy said. As the judge, she absolutely had to have one—and Ray would need something too, for being the announcer. They crawled out of their hideout and started back up to the house. Veddy had pulled the limo up under the portico, and as they approached, they saw Marietta and Lionel come out the front door and climb in. Ray and Ivy watched as Veddy drove off, down the long tongue of the driveway.

"Where do you think they go?" Ray wondered, nodding toward the back of the limo.

"Probably looking for other families to wreck," Ivy said. "Other kids to steal." She dug her heels into the lawn as she made her way up the hill. "They probably have a ring," she said.

"A ring?" Ray said.

"And Marietta's the ringleader," Ivy continued. "And Veddy is her accomplice!" That's what they had called Carol during the trial: Dan's accomplice. "And so is Sissy! They're *all* guilty!" Ivy declared, and thinking about it made her walk faster, on a mission to find herself a robe.

Inside, they went straight to their closets to see if they had anything good. Ray settled on the yellow Boston Bruins windbreaker, no. 11, that had been packed inside his suitcase, and that was actually too small for him. But there was nothing right for Ivy. The towels in the bathroom were big enough to drape around her, but the wrong color altogether—a soft blue she said was for babies.

"What about the sheet?" Ray said. "From the picture."

Ah! The black sheet that covered the painting in the hall! An ocean of material she could wrap herself in. It was such a good idea she was sorry she hadn't thought of it herself, but she had to hand it to Ray. "Good surveillance," she told him, even though technically they had surveilled it the day before.

They walked back into the dim hallway, down to the darkest end, where the covered painting hung. They could unhook the sheet from the bottom, freeing the fancy gold frame beneath, but it was too high up for them to reach the top. They went back to their bedrooms and dragged down their desk chairs to use as stepladders, for extra height.

Then, with everything in place for disrobing the painting, they stood still by the chairs and didn't move. They looked at the shrouded painting and then at each other.

"Why do you think they covered it up?" Ray asked.

Hadn't he asked her that before? Ivy hadn't known then, and she didn't know now. She hated not knowing.

"Dare me?" she asked. If Ivy got dared, she did it no matter what.

"Dare you," Ray said.

Those good old words! "But you have to help," Ivy said. "Do your side." She climbed up onto the chair.

Ray still didn't move. "What if Marietta catches us?" he said.

"She's gone," Ivy said. "And besides, she doesn't even come down here. This end is for servants," she said. "C'mon. You dared me."

So Ray climbed onto his chair too, and they pulled up the sides of the sheet as far as they could, straining to unhook it at the top. Ivy started fanning the material until it puffed out like a sail. "Harder," she said, pumping the sheet in and out. Finally it filled with enough air to carry it off Ivy's corner, and they were able to swing the whole thing to the side and release it entirely. It went sailing and settled on the floor in an elegant heap. Ray and Ivy were still standing on the chairs, so close to the painting that all they could really see were blocks of color and brushstrokes.

They climbed down and backed up to take a look. It was just another man, but younger, dressed in some sort of uniform, holding a hat under his arm.

Ray and Ivy stared and stared. There was nothing *wrong* with the painting, but something was funny about it. Maybe because, unlike the people in all the other portraits, the man in this one was smiling—or actually, Ivy thought, he was smirking.

"Who is it?" Ray asked, and Ivy felt like she *almost* had an answer, but it wouldn't pop out of her mouth. She stepped closer to the picture to examine the little gold rectangle set in the bottom of the frame: BLACK-STONE MOUTON III. "Blackstone Mouton

Eye Eye Eye," she read aloud. She turned to Ray and shrugged. "Another dumb relative," she said. Then she leaned over and grabbed the sheet. Trailing black silk, they ran down the hall to Ivy's bedroom, where they closed the door behind them.

There, in her room, Ivy could fully appreciate what they had snatched: the miles and miles of material, shiny and silky, perfect for wrapping around and draping herself in. She covered herself in its folds, adjusted an end over her shoulder like a toga, gave it a little flip.

Ray's voice came to her out of nowhere. "Ivy?" he said.

She stopped her primping and looked at him, standing there in his Bruins windbreaker with the sleeves pulling up from his wrists, eyeing her robe.

"Let's take turns being the judge," he said.

She was stung by his suggestion but had to agree. "OK," she said reluctantly. "But I'm first."

They decided to hold the trial in the bathroom. Ivy wanted to make an entrance from her room, and judge from the bathtub in her bare feet and her robe.

"We'll just do the sentencing part today, since we

don't have all the stuff we need for a real trial," she said. "Yet," she added.

"Who'll we sentence?" Ray said.

"I'll sentence you and then you can do me," Ivy said.

But once she got in the tub and had Ray stand up on the toilet seat, she had no desire to punish him. She couldn't even call him guilty. They stood there staring at each other.

"Let's do the dolls instead," she said. Why not? There were a ton of them in her room, just sitting there.

They went and turned the key that opened the door to the collection. It was a world of dolls—one from every country Ivy had ever heard of, and some that she hadn't, each one in a different costume, all of them mounted on wire stands that stuck up under their clothes. "C'mon," Ivy told Ray, grabbing a few. All their clothes felt starchy, nothing she wanted to hold close. "Bring in a bunch," Ivy said. She placed the first one on the closed toilet seat—Miss Portugal—and set the others in the sink. "We'll do one at a time," she said.

When they had the sink loaded, Ivy went back into her bedroom and closed the door. Ray was going to count to twenty and then call out, "All rise." Just before

she swept in, Ivy grabbed the key from the cabinet—
she needed something she could tap with—and then,
on Ray's cue, she entered. She climbed back into the

tub and clanged the key against the faucet. The sound it made wasn't bad at all, and she called out, "This court is in order." Then she sentenced Miss Portugal to ten years in jail, and clanged with her key again. Ray whisked the doll from the toilet seat and carried her off to the cabinet. He was back a second later, looking for the key so he could lock her up.

"But bring it back," Ivy called after him. She needed it for clanging.

When Ray returned, he plucked Miss Uruguay from the sink for sentencing.

Ivy gave her three years and Ray locked her up.

Miss France got ten. Miss Argentina, in her tango dress, twenty-five. Ivy gave Miss Canada life.

Miss Guinea was up when Ivy and Ray heard a car. Ray ran to the window and saw the limo.

"Quick," Ivy said, climbing out of the tub, already unwrapping her robe. Ray came over to help spin her out, but she told him to get all the dolls locked up first. She hadn't even had a chance to officially adjourn court.

By the time Ray had all the dolls back in place, Ivy's robe was a mound of black sheet on the floor.

"I didn't get my turn," Ray said.

"Next time," Ivy promised him. "If Marietta catches us, she'll throw the book at us."

"Put us in jail?" Ray asked, his eyes big.

"Kids don't," Ivy said, in a hurry. "Go to jail. But we have to get rid of the evidence. C'mon."

They dragged the sheet out into the hallway and tiptoed forward, as if the men in the paintings were sleeping and could be woken up. Ivy was looking at Eye Eye Eye, step by step getting closer.

"Hey, Ray," she said, stopping suddenly. "Look at his face. Dontcha think he kinda looks like Dan?"

"Dan?" Ray said. "*Our* Dan?" He stretched his neck to consider.

And then Ivy could see that he saw the resemblance, too. It dawned all over his face.

Ray turned to her with big eyes. "How come?" he said.

Ivy studied the painting again. There was definitely a resemblance, and she didn't like it one bit. "It's like she's stealing our whole family," Ivy said. She remembered what her father had called Marietta. He had called her a witch.

But she didn't have time to worry right then and there. They had to get the picture covered back up. The last thing on earth they wanted was to have Marietta catch them.

Ivy and Ray spent the rest of the day outside. They practiced for their midnight moonlight race in the garden, and they drew up a floor plan of the house, and they rescued a shoebox from the trash to hold valuables and evidence in their hideout. Because Ray begged to, they spied into the garage and caught Veddy with his jacket off, polishing the limousine.

That night, their second at the big house, Ray fell asleep right away, before they even whistled back and forth at all. But Ivy couldn't. She was worried. About that portrait in the hall and how come it looked like Dan. *Was* Marietta a witch? she wondered. Was *that* the answer? She worried about the stupid picture in the newspaper, too, and what it said about Ray and her being lost. She worried Ray would wet the bed again. Sometimes when the rain in Spain got started it rained for a while. And since she was worrying anyway, she worried about how long twenty-five years was. She wanted her parents to escape, somehow, or even better, she wanted to rescue them. And of course she wanted a hammer, just like the judge's. But most of all, more than anything, so much she could barely stand it right at that second, she wanted her mother. She pictured her just the way she had seen her at the end, in court, standing to receive her sentence. Ivy didn't even need her to turn around—she couldn't have stood that—so when she thought about her, she just thought of the back of her, standing, and her curls and the glint of red in her hair.

She stretched herself out in the bed. Even making herself as long as she could, and flinging her arms out wide, like a snow angel, she still took up only a fraction of the mattress. It seemed like a waste of space, just like the whole big house was. Ray could have fit in her bed with her, no problem. They could have shared a room, like they always had before, in all the different places they had lived. She told herself it would be a whole lot easier for her to watch her brother's back if she could see it.

Ivy climbed out of her big, high bed and tiptoed into the bathroom. The tiles were cool against the bottom of her bare feet. She stood on the threshold of Ray's room and studied the still lump under his covers. "Ray," she whispered. "Ray." He didn't stir. She hissed louder, "Ray," and he still didn't wake up. She stepped quietly into his room and went over to his bed and stared at him, but nothing. Finally she went around to the other side of his bed and climbed in next to him, and then she was asleep in no time.

The Intercom

During the night the rain in Spain fell in torrents. The next morning Ray and Ivy woke up at just about the same time and hopped out of their wet bed.

"I'm sorry," Ray mumbled miserably from his side.

"*Don't* be sorry," she ordered, as if she was mad—and she *was* mad, but not at him. "You didn't do anything *wrong*," she decreed. She immediately started yanking at the sheets and balling them up. Sheets had never before seemed so massive, so voluminous. She was thinking up ways to get rid of the evidence when Sissy came into the bedroom and saw them and got her end-of-the-world face.

"Please don't tell," Ivy said, trailing along behind her. "Please don't. We'll be your best friends," she promised. When that didn't get a response, Ivy kept right on going. She knew, from playing poker, what it meant to up the ante. "We'll pay you," she said. "We'll do your work. We'll be your *slaves*," she offered. But Sissy didn't seem to hear a word Ivy was saying. She gathered the ball of sheets in her arms and hurried out the door.

Ray and Ivy were left, again, with only each other.

"What do you think she'll do?" Ray said.

"Sissy?" Ivy said.

"No," Ray moaned. He looked nailed to the floor with dread. "Marietta."

"Oh, don't worry about *her*," Ivy said. But she had the exact same worry inside her own head.

"She said if it happened again something would have to be *done*, remember?"

Of course Ivy remembered. She walked over to her brother. She looked at him hard, right in the eyes. And even though she was looking at his face she felt for sure that she was watching his back when she promised him, "Whatever it is, we'll be OK. We'll fix it. We'll get the better of her. She's met her *match*," Ivy proclaimed, and even just saying so buoyed her spirits. She led Ray down the grand staircase to breakfast with head held high.

They took their seats on either side of Marietta. Lionel, magnifying glass in hand, sat hunched in his place, far away. Sissy, nervous as ever, entered with the tray and delivered Marietta's egg in its holder along with her weapon for beheading it. Then she turned to serve Ivy, who helped herself to plenty of bacon; she was already better at using the fancy silver tongs. They gave her a sudden stab of memory, though: of eating takeout Chinese with Dan, and how really good he was with chopsticks.

Ray passed on the bacon but took cereal and berries, and then, just when everyone was poised to dig in—Marietta had the clipper positioned on the top of her egg—Marietta announced that in light of the most recent mishap she would be moving Ray downstairs, to the small room just off the kitchen, adjacent to the laundry.

"What?" Ivy yelped. The word popped out of her mouth even though words didn't, usually, around Marietta.

"A simple necessity," Marietta continued, "if there is to be the daily laundering of messed sheets."

Ivy hated that word—*messed*. She sounded like she was talking about a dog. Did she think Ray was a dog? Ray was a boy, Ray was her brother! Ivy couldn't even stand to look across the table at him, to see his red ears. She looked down at her plate. There was the bacon, but gone was her appetite: another breakfast down the tubes.

"Andrew will move your things," Marietta finished. (Andrew, Ivy realized, was Marietta's name for Veddy.) Then she lowered the cutter over her egg and squeezed the handles together. The small circle of teeth appeared and cut into the shell. Despite their misery at the news she had just delivered, Ray and Ivy couldn't help leaning in closer to watch, spellbound.

"What is it?" Marietta said when she looked up and caught them gazing so intently. "Didn't anyone ever teach you it's impolite to stare?"

Both Ray and Ivy pulled back and looked away and shook their heads no.

"Oh, Lionel," she called down to the other end of the table, "they're little *savages*."

Ray and Ivy headed down to their hideout, their hearts so heavy they didn't even run. Ray wasn't saying a word, and Ivy was scared to look at him. Sometimes seeing Ray's face killed her. It showed everything. Ivy had what her father called a poker face, meaning that you couldn't always tell by looking at it what she was feeling or thinking. But Ray was the opposite.

She finally stole a look, and his face was as sad as she knew it would be. He had to be thinking the same things she was: No more secret passageway. The downstairs a million miles away. The two of them apart. *Solitary confinement!*

"We'll make a plan," Ivy announced. "We'll send messages to each other." She had watched a movie with Dan once where prisoners in stone cells tapped out messages to each other with rocks.

Ray's face instantly turned hopeful. "How?" he said.

She didn't know, exactly. "Maybe like an intercom,"

she said. Once her father had rented office space to work out of for a few weeks and Carol played his secretary and they used intercoms to talk to each other without opening their doors. "We'll dope it out," she said, like her father always did. "All we need is a good idea."

"A lucky break," Ray chimed in.

"Yeah," Ivy said. "Let's go to the pergola."

It was splendid out—not even Marietta could wreck the good weather—and the gardens were going strong. They sat on a bench in the midst of tall stalks loaded with flowers. Different scents blew over them whenever there was a breeze. They sat in silence, staring up at the big house, waiting for an idea to come. They watched as Veddy pulled the limo under the portico and Marietta emerged and the two of them drove off.

"Good riddance," Ivy said.

After a while Ray asked, "Where *is* my new room?" He was studying the vast expanse of the building.

Ivy pointed to a small window, almost like a ship portal, on the lower left side. "Down there, I think."

"Under yours?" he said.

Ray was right: Ivy's left window was directly above Ray's, only higher—Ivy estimated about half a mile.

And as soon as Ivy saw that, she saw possibilities. She pictured a ladder shooting straight up from the top of Ray's window to the bottom of hers. Or maybe a slide, straight out of hers and down into Ray's; or a pole, like in a firehouse. Even just a long rope—a cabin they stayed at for part of one summer had been on a lake, and the way to get into the lake was to swing out over it on a thick braided rope that hung from a tree's high branch, and just let go. Ivy and Ray had swung off it a million times. There was no reason—none—that Ray's room and hers couldn't still be connected, no matter what Marietta had decreed.

All they really needed to hatch their plan was rope, and so they snuck out back, to where Sissy had hung out Ray's sheets for the whole world to see the day before. She didn't have them hanging out yet, this morning. "We have to work fast," Ivy told Ray. But the line was tied too high up on the pole for them to reach. "Here," Ivy said, and she made a stirrup with her linked hands and bent down and gave Ray a lift. "Hurry it up," she told him. "My fingers are breaking. I can't hold forever."

Finally Ray got the knot untied, and the clothesline came free and swung down to where Ivy could reach it.

She unwrapped it from the pole and then around her bent elbow and in between her thumb and the rest of her fingers. For just a moment she felt like a cowboy with a lasso, from all the Westerns she had watched with Dan on TV. "OK," she said when she had a good long piece of line bundled up.

Ray was standing still. "What if Sissy tells?" he said.

Ivy held still herself for a moment. "Tells what?" she said. "That her clothesline is gone?"

Ray nodded, eyes big.

"Well, they're not gonna suspect *us*," she said indignantly. "What would *we* want with a stupid clothesline?"

Ray still looked worried.

"Look," she told her brother, "all Sissy's gonna do

when she finds her clothesline missing is cry about it. Now c'mon," she said, and led him around to the back door.

They peeked to make sure the coast was clear in the kitchen. Sissy was gone, and they tiptoed inside. Ray went to his new bedroom downstairs and Ivy upstairs to hers, and then, with Ivy up above and Ray directly below, they proceeded to build another kind of clothesline, only they rigged this one to run up and down instead of side to side, looping the rope through the shutter latches on their windows and tying it taut to make a perfect little relay between their two positions.

Ivy already had something in mind for what they could use to hold their messages. She found the bag of marbles that had been packed in her ratty suitcase, and emptied the marbles into her dresser drawer. There was a muffled rumbling as she pushed the drawer shut and took the pouch over to the window and attached it to the clothesline by its rawhide drawstring.

"Just a sec," she called down to Ray, and went to her desk for paper and pencil. She considered, then, exactly what to say in the very first note that would travel via their intercom. She knew it wouldn't matter that much to Ray—he couldn't really read yet, and still wrote his name backwards—but it mattered to her. She wanted the words to be right. A moment later she wrote, *We Win!*, and she signed both their names. As she was about to stuff it into the pouch, though, she reconsidered, worried about what could happen if the note got intercepted. She had watched a spy movie with Dan once, late at night, where the spy got caught carrying a secret message. He tried to hide the message by eating it, but the bad guys got it before he could swallow and then dragged him off to a basement and hung him by his thumbs. Ivy ripped up her first note into tiny pieces and shoved them deep into her pocket. On a new piece of paper she wrote, again, *We Win*, but this time she didn't sign any names. Instead, she drew a big eye, perfectly almond-shaped with a large pupil and five long, curved eyelashes. She would be The Eye.

Ivy popped the note into the leather pouch, tightened it at the top, and sent the message on its way, pulling on the line until it looped around to Ray's window. Looking down, she could see his little hand reaching out to get it.

A few seconds later he called up to her, "What's it say?"

"'We win,'" she hollered down. "Send one to me,"

she told him, "but don't sign your name. Make a picture. That way they'll never identify us in a court of law." Ray was gone from the window, but she kept calling out directions. "In case our notes get *intercepted*," she said, delighted at how the word simply rolled off her tongue—a word, she thought, every bit as good as *pergola*. Ray didn't holler back up, asking her what it meant, but she acted as if he had. "Intercepted means if you don't have time to eat them," she called out her window.

Finally she saw Ray's head; he was stuffing his response into the pouch, and pulling the clothes-

line to send it up to her. It worked beautifully, their contraption. But as she watched the pouch inching its way toward her, she thought of something that would make it even better.

Ivy plucked Ray's note from the marble bag. On the other side of the message Ivy had sent to him, he had drawn a sun, big lines shooting out from a small circle.

"Good sign," Ivy shouted down. They untied the line then, and Ivy hauled the whole thing in through her window and stored it away in her bottom dresser drawer. They had decided to use their intercom only at night, when they really needed it, and so they wouldn't get caught.

A minute later they had reconvened on the middle step of the back staircase.

"It should make a sound," she told Ray. "So we can hear the message coming. Then it would be perfect."

"We could knock," Ray suggested. "On the wall."

"A *better* sound," Ivy insisted, and she had no sooner said it than she knew what she was after, the *exact* sound she wanted to hear: "Marietta's *jewelry*!" she cried. She was remembering the soft tinkle of Marietta's charm bracelet as she sat on the stand pointing at Dan, and as she led Ray and Ivy down the hallway that first day in the big house. What a rich little jingle those charms made—exactly the sound their intercom deserved. Plus they could just clip it right onto the clothesline. "Let's sneak out some of her jewelry," she suggested.

"Steal?" Ray said.

"Not *steal*," Ivy corrected. She was indignant. "We *need* the bracelet," she explained. "For something *good*."

"What if Marietta finds out?" Ray said.

"Oh, Ray," Ivy said. "Marietta's rich. She probably has *tons* of bracelets. She's not gonna notice just one." Then Ivy reminded Ray what an excellent sneaker he was, and she had him enlisted in no time.

They went to the top of the stairs and looked down the long hallway, from the East Wing into the dark tunnel of Marietta and Lionel's West Wing. Even though no one was around, they tiptoed the whole way, past their bedroom doors, past the grand staircase, into unknown territory. Ivy's heart was hammering. The first room they came to on their right was another shiny bathroom, this one big enough to drive a little car into. The toilet had railings on either side of it that made Ivy think of monkeybars on the playground.

The next room down the hallway was so filled up with furniture—couches and tables—that Ivy thought at first it was another living room. She and Ray tiptoed in. A curvy little couch covered in red velvet caught Ivy's eye, especially the long, satiny fringe all around its base. Ivy felt she was looking at the kind of furniture that if you lay down on it a servant would appear and bring you whatever you wanted. She could imagine herself sprawled out on it, head resting on the cross-stitched pillow that, in letters made out of a million tiny x's, said *Where there's a will there's a way*—just like the footstool in the living room.

Ray didn't give the couch a second glance; he tip-toed deeper into the room, and when Ivy saw what he was after, she forgot all about the couch and the pillow and joined him. He was headed straight toward the long, low dresser of many drawers, with a fancy box sitting on top. They reached for the box and lifted its lid, opening to velvet-lined drawers filled with jewelry, all the bracelets neatly laid out in their own section as if they had been put to bed. Quick as a blink Ivy had what she wanted in her hand—the one with all the charms attached to it. Ray lowered the lid and they stepped away. And then they turned and froze dead in their tracks.

There, set back at the far other end of the room, in a huge bed that looked like a sleigh, was Lionel!— propped up in bed against a mountain of pillows, his eyes closed, his limbs motionless. His magnifying glass lay beside him on the covers, next to the little lump his body made. He looked dead—dead as a doornail, Ivy thought. She and Ray turned to each other with huge eyes. Then, in the slowest motion, as silent as could be, they started backing up, step by step by step, never taking their eyes from the little man in the big bed, until they had backed straight out the door they'd just entered. And once they were standing in the hallway again, they let out the breath they'd been holding and then they took off, shooting past the bathroom, the staircase, their own bedroom doors, down the back staircase, and out the kitchen door, letting it slam behind them as they made a beeline down to their hideout, Marietta's jewelry jingling in Ivy's hot little hands.

They crawled inside and sat cross-legged, panting, beneath the umbrella of branches, for a long time.

"Do you think," Ivy said finally, "do you think...he was *dead*?"

How big Ray's eyes got told Ivy that he hadn't thought that at all.

"He's not," she said quickly. "He just *looked* kind of dead."

"I thought he was asleep," Ray said.

"He was," Ivy agreed. "Asleep." She knew that. And she was glad Ray knew it, because otherwise it would really have scared him. "Good thing he didn't see us," she said.

Ray nodded. "Whadoyou think he'd do?" he said. "If he caught us?"

Ivy considered. "Not *chase* us," she said, and they both laughed at the thought of Lionel hobbling after them down the hall. "With his magnifying glass," Ivy said, and she held up her hand as if she had one, and they laughed more.

"He'd probably just tell Marietta," Ray said, and that got them quiet. "What do you think *she'd* do?" Ray said. "If she caught us?"

"Oh," Ivy said, "she'd *accuse* us." The thought of it made her indignant. "*Charge* us. Get us *sent away*." The courtroom words just rolled off her tongue.

"Up the river?" Ray asked, big-eyed.

"Yeah," she agreed, before she looked at his face. "But kids don't," she reminded him quickly. "Get sent to jail. And besides," Ivy added, opening her fist to the mound of bracelet and charms, "she didn't—catch us."

That night, at bedtime, they hooked up their intercom and attached the jingling jewelry and sent messages filled with eyes and suns to each other. A milky, egg-shaped moon was perched right outside their windows, and in between notes Ivy gave serious consideration to the midnight race they would run when it was full. She had never really paid much attention to the moon before—she'd never had a good reason to—but now she studied with deep interest its size and veins and contours, the light it cast over everything. Ivy took it as another good sign that the moon rose where she and Ray could keep an eye on it. Was it getting smaller? she wondered. Or bigger? She couldn't really tell which way things were going. But her question gave her a good idea.

From that night on, Ray and Ivy sketched the moon. In the morning they smuggled their pictures down to their hideout to examine in the light of day. They saved all their drawings in the shoebox. The pictures didn't prove anyone was guilty, but Ivy said they constituted real evidence—information that told them just how close they were coming to their biggest and best race yet.

And on the very first night that their intercom was up and running, and for many nights that followed, the rain in Spain didn't fall, not a drop.

Dares

"Ut-way oo-day oo-yay unt-way oo-tay oo-day?" Ivy asked.

"Ut-way oo-day *oo-yay* unt-way oo-tay oo-day?" Ray answered.

They were up in Ivy's room. She had been writing out the notes they would send to each other when the moon was completely full and it was time to run their midnight race, and Ray was signing them with suns and eyes. But they had done that for a while. They were bored.

"We should get more evidence against Marietta," Ivy said. She felt like they had kind of slacked off on that front. "Have to keep our eyes on the prize," she said: something else her father had taught her.

"What prize?"

"Marietta!" Ivy said. "Get her back for what she did."

"Oh," Ray said. He didn't care so much about getting back at people. "Let's do something with the limousine," he suggested.

"Can't," Ivy said. "The old man's snoring"—which is what they said in their family whenever it was raining out, pouring. "Has to be an inside job," she told him, and just a second later she got a great idea. "The cake!" she said.

"The cake?" Ray said.

"Let's get the paper out of that glass tube," she said. "It's gotta be a document—it's rolled up. And documents are *definitely* evidence."

"The cake that's under the *glass*?" Ray said.

"Yeah," Ivy said. "With the document." She was nodding slowly as a whole, beautiful plan filled her mind. "And all we have to do is lift the lid!"

They stuffed the notes they'd been working on into their pockets and went downstairs via the grand staircase. "You have to help me," Ivy told Ray. She told him more than once.

The entryway was empty and no one else was around. Veddy had chauffeured Marietta off somewhere right after breakfast, and they could imagine where Lionel was: back in bed, asleep, his magnifying glass by his side. Ivy said Sissy was probably off crying somewhere—crying and cleaning one of the hundred rooms in the house.

Ray and Ivy cross-stepped their way over the diamond-shaped tiles to stand on opposite sides of the domed cake. The glass cover, fragile and formidable at the same time, spanned the replica of the big house, the carved bride and groom on top, and, in front, on its wire stand, the silver-handled glass tube. Something else was underneath the dome, too, Ivy knew—the spider—but she told herself not to think about that.

"OK," she said, spreading out her hands in the air, "OK." She was racing inside. This was it. "Dare me?" she asked.

"Dare you," Ray answered, those magic words. They bolstered her every time—set her on a mission, a quest. They practically put her on a horse!

"Reach under on your side," she told Ray, as she felt along the base for some place to get a grip. Suddenly her fingers slipped into an indentation in the glass just meant for hands. "Ha!" she cried out in delight. The built-in lifters felt like an invitation to Ivy, asking her—*calling* on her—to please keep going, to raise up that lid and get the prize!

"Ready?" she asked Ray, looking at his face through the glass. His eyes were big and round. Ivy loved that face.

He nodded, hands in place.

"One, two, three," they counted together, and then they both lifted up. Slowly, uncertainly, the glass dome rose, rose, rocking back and forth between them. It wasn't terribly heavy, but it was cumbersome to navigate up and over the cake. "Higher," Ivy directed. They had to clear the bride and the groom before they could move the dome sideways and down, and Ray was stretched almost as far as he could stretch already. "Just a little bit more, a little bit higher," Ivy urged. They both gave it their best shot, but even so they nicked the very top of the carved figures, pushing them forward into the frosting, so they looked poised to dive into one of the cake's lower layers.

Ivy kept right on going, though. She and Ray had the dome over the top of the cake and were lowering it down between them. "Over here," Ivy directed, and she and Ray shuffled along as best they could, crouching to set it down at the base of the stairs. "Careful," Ivy kept saying. "Careful, careful." She didn't want it to shatter across the floor. She and Ray had dropped glass things before.

But now they had it within an inch of the tiled floor. They counted together, just as they had for the liftoff, and on three they set the glass lid down with a satisfying click at precisely the same time. They slowly withdrew their hands and leaned away from it, and only then breathed in a deep breath. Done!

They went straight back to the cake.

How different everything looked to Ivy without its glass protection: the miniature big house, and the bride and groom, and the scroll resting on its little holder. How was it, she wondered, that a see-through ceiling could make such a difference, keep so separate what was really there beneath it? There was no doubt now that she was close to the real things. She put her face right up to the hardened, granular frosting, so close to the tilted bride and groom that she could see the swirly grain of wood on their faces. And the top hat! It was even better than she remembered it being, better than it had appeared under glass. It was perfectly shaped and very small, and its black silk gleamed a little. Without thought, without plan, her hand rose as if on its own, and in the next instant, with just a pinch, she held the perfect thing in her fingers. A particular thrill of satisfaction flooded Ivy as she examined it—this object that she had seen and wanted and up until that moment had not had.

"Hey!" Ray said.

His voice startled Ivy. She had forgotten him, that he was there; she had forgotten everything.

"I thought we were getting a document."

"We are," she said. "We are." The silk hat, light as a breath, rested on her palm, a jewel. "*And* the hat," she said.

"Is it evidence?" Ray asked.

Ivy swallowed. "Sure," she said. "Sure it's evidence."

"Lemme see," he said, and held out his hand.

She didn't want to let it go. But she had to—they were in on this together, and it was only fair. She rolled the top hat into Ray's hand for him to inspect. Then she straightened the hatless groom and the bride with the bleeding lipstick. They sank a little deeper into the crusty frosting, but at least she got them standing at attention.

Finally Ivy lifted the glass cylinder off its wire holder—to get the document they had come for. The tube was made of plastic, though, not glass—it reminded her of a snow dome she got one time at a hotel gift shop in Las Vegas—and it was stoppered at both ends with corks topped with silver pulls. She yanked out one of the corks and, using her fingers like pincers, extracted the rolled parchment from the tube.

Just as she was about to unfurl it, to see how good a document it really was, they heard a distant roaring, coming from upstairs. They startled, then froze. "Vacuum cleaner," Ray said— making its way down the hallway. Was it coming closer or moving away? Just as with the moon, Ivy couldn't tell. But it didn't matter—it was time for their getaway.

She pushed the rolled parchment through the belt loop of her shorts and re-stoppered the cylinder and set it back on its wire stand. She reached over

to Ray and grabbed the top hat and shoved it deep into her pocket. "C'mon," she told him, heading over to the glass dome, motioning for him to take his place on the other side. "Hurry up."

They hoisted on the count of three, and gave the cover a fairly smooth liftoff. They took baby steps back to the table and managed to tilt and lift the dome, stretching, stretching over the carved figures, and then shakily, wobbly, lowering it down. "OK," Ivy hummed, "OK, OK, OK." They had it within an inch of the table, almost there.

But that's when she saw it, or thought she saw it—saw *something*. Out of the corner of her eye. The spider? What else could it have been? Something quick and dark that startled her and made her jump back, yank her fingers away from the cake and what she happened to be holding, so that her side of the dome landed first, settling just a fraction of a second before Ray—who held on to his side until the very end—let go. And then: a quick, sharp sound—a snap, almost—and Ivy watched in utter horror as a fine crack shot through the glass, starting just above the indentation and traveling up before her, a fork of lightning, appearing but then not *dis*appearing: *there*.

The sound that came out of Ivy's mouth was a crack all its own.

"What?" Ray said. "What, Ivy?" He came running around to see.

Ivy turned on him in a fury. "See what you made me do?" she hissed.

"Me?" Ray practically squealed. "*I* didn't do it."

Ivy panicked. It was like the time she and Ray had spilled an entire bottle of ink—all over a fancy leather blotter in the principal's office. "C'mon," she said. "We have to fix it."

"How do we fix it?"

The crack, the bit of lightning in the glass, loomed before Ivy, all she could see. It wasn't just big; it was everything. "Maybe if we turned it around," she said. She thought maybe it wouldn't be so noticeable on the other side. But what if the dome broke when they lifted it? Wasn't a crack just a hair away from a break? She imagined the whole thing shattering even as they held it. And the vacuum cleaner was coming! How close *was* Sissy? "No," she said. "We can't risk it."

"We could put a sheet over it," Ray suggested. "Like the picture upstairs."

"Oh, Ray," Ivy sang out, dancing her feet up and down in despair. "Then she'd *really* notice it." They couldn't lift it up or turn it around or cover it with a black cloth. They had to live with it.

She stepped back, walked around in a small circle a couple of times, and then looked at it again. The crack wasn't *that* big, she told herself. "Here," she said, "help me twist the table a little," and she and Ray angled the table so the cracked side of the dome was turned closer to the wall. Then Ivy and Ray walked over by the steps.

"You can't even see it from here," Ray said.

"Yeah," Ivy agreed. Her heart was finally pounding a little less.

They took tiny steps away from the staircase, gauging how far they could go before they saw the crack.

When they finally did see it, and from a distance, it really wasn't very big at all. Especially if they squinted.

"She'll never notice it," Ivy declared. "She's practically blind anyway."

"Marietta's blind?" Ray said.

"Well, *Lionel* is," Ivy said. "That's close enough."

Minutes later they were sitting cross-legged in their hideout. What a relief, after everything that had happened, to reconvene there, beneath the leafy umbrella, in its cool, dim envelope of roots and branches. Ivy called the meeting to order, and then they sat without saying anything, a little stunned. It had been a big morning.

The document was still tucked through Ivy's belt loop, poking her in the side a little, and finally she pulled it out and held it between Ray and her. "Our ill-gotten gain," she said respectfully. Oh, how she missed her father! She started to unroll the paper. She felt like she should be dressed up in tights and velvet, and standing in a castle, about to read a message from the king—a matter of life and death. She cleared her throat.

"Is it a map?" Ray blurted, leaning closer.

No, it wasn't a map. But there were two pieces of paper, one inside the other. "We hit the jackpot!" Ivy declared. The heavier paper, with swirly letters in gold across the top, proclaimed itself the certificate of marriage of Lionel Noland and Marietta Mouton and was covered with fancy lettering. "That's what I call a document!" Ivy said proudly. And then, with even greater excitement, she unrolled the second paper. It wasn't parchment, just regular white paper with lots of typing on it.

"Last Will and Testa," Ivy sounded out. "Ment."

"What's that?"

Ivy didn't know. She was scanning down the fine print, but it was filled with a thousand words she would have to sound out to pronounce—almost but not quite another language.

"Is it top secret?" Ray asked—the next best thing to a map.

She was studying the wobbly signature at the bottom of the page. "Oh, brother," she groaned, and her hopeful shoulders dropped. "It's not even *Marietta's* document," she said. "Look—it's signed by Blackstone Mouton." She held the paper out to Ray, disgusted.

Ray pored over it as if he could read. "Can it still be evidence?" he asked.

Ivy thought how Ray just didn't get it, what was evidence and what wasn't. But she didn't want to hurt his feelings. "We'll keep it in the shoebox anyway," she told him. She let go of the bottom of the paper and it rolled up on itself, and she tossed it into the box. "At least we got the marriage certificate," she said.

"And the hat," Ray said. "*That's* evidence—you said so."

The hat! She had forgotten all about it. Now she reached into her side pocket and pulled it out, along with a spray of crumpled notes. They both leaned in to examine it on her palm.

"*How* is it?" Ray asked.

"What?"

"Evidence."

Ivy paused. "Well," she said.

"What's it prove?"

Ivy set it in the shoebox, next to the curled-up will and testament, and their ball of silver foil, and the Lost Children picture from the newspaper, and their drawings of the moon. "Well," she said again. "It proves I did your dare and lifted the lid."

"What else?" Ray asked.

"It proves," she said again. "Oh, Ray," she finally said, exasperated. "Sometimes you don't know till the end what things prove. That's why they have trials."

Zapped

"The summer is *flying* by," Marietta announced at breakfast a few days later. "It will be gone before we know it."

She was talking to the air, as always. Ray and Ivy were eating and Lionel was looking at the paper through his magnifying glass.

"So it's time," she continued, "to decide where I'll be sending you off to school. Broken Sparrow Academy has openings, I believe."

Ray and Ivy got suddenly still. The thought of getting sent away by Marietta sickened Ivy—as much as, or even more than, school itself. She and Ray had served time in a bunch of different schools and had never liked any of them. Besides, it was *summer*; why was Marietta even *talking* about school? She and Ray exchanged looks across the table—miserable little looks.

"May we be excused?" Ivy said feebly. Barely a bite of bacon and Marietta had once again stolen her appetite.

"Go," and Marietta fluttered her fingers at them. "Play," she told them. "While you still have the chance."

"What's a cademy?" Ray wanted to know as soon as they were in their hideout, before Ivy had even called the meeting to order.

"Another name for school," she answered him. She knew because once her family—oh, her family! Even to think of them gave her a pang—had lived next door to the Tres Chic Beauty Academy, run by their neighbor, DeeAnna D'Argent. "'Member that brick building next to the apartment?" she asked Ray. "That smelled funny inside?"

But he didn't remember; he'd been too little, just a baby.

"Anyway," she said, "that was one." Not that Marietta was going to send them away to cut hair—Ivy didn't believe that for a minute. She just didn't know *what* Marietta had up her sleeve.

"Never mind," Ivy said. "Forget about it." She didn't want Ray worrying about school, now that the rain in Spain had stopped falling. "We have all summer," she reminded him. "*Our* summer doesn't have to fly by just because Marietta's is."

But Marietta made it hard for them to forget about it. She brought up Broken Sparrow Academy almost daily—one morning a word about applications, the next about interviews, soon she was talking *deadlines.* And then she delivered the deadliest news of all: she was going to have them tested. "We need to know what—if *anything*—we have to work with," she announced.

"What *kind* of test?" Ivy said. Her stomach had drained down to the bottom of her feet, which weren't swinging.

"Comprehensive," Marietta sniffed.

Ivy didn't even know what comprehensive *was.* And she hated getting things wrong. And Ray! He hated *any* kind of test. They made him sick, especially timed tests in arithmetic.

"When?" Ivy said weakly. She felt like she had asked to hear their own sentence.

"At my convenience," Marietta answered, and that was that. Ivy thought she heard the faint echo of the hammer falling, and then Marietta dismissed them, as she always did.

On their way down to the hideout Ray asked her, "Do we *have* to take the test?"

Ivy knew what his face looked like even without looking at it: the way it looked when he had to get a shot. "We'll review," she told him. "I'll be the teacher." She'd go over everything she could remember from first and second grade. "Addition and subtraction," she said. She wouldn't bother with spelling, which she'd never had any luck with.

That night, with every message she sent down via the intercom, she included a math problem. She made sure to use lots of 11's and 7's, 7 and 11 being known lucky numbers. Ray got three in a row right, and Ivy thought that was a good note on which to end their day.

Ivy woke up the next morning to the jingle-jangle of their intercom. It was early.

She slipped out of bed and ran to the window. Ray was sending up a note, even though they usually didn't

before breakfast—that's when they unhooked the clothesline and hid it away. The bracelet looked nice, though; it caught the sun and sparkled as it traveled up the side of the house.

She pinched the folded paper out of the little pouch. Ray's sun signature was on one side, and on the other he'd drawn a massive number of short lines, little dashes, all slanted in one direction. She leaned out the window and looked down.

"It's the rain," he called up to her. "In Spain."

She looked again at the note in her hand: the rain,

of course, in Spain. It had fallen, she realized—why wouldn't it, with comprehensive testing breathing down their necks?

She threw on her clothes and headed down to Ray's room via the back stairway. Sissy was at the stove frying bacon. Ivy headed straight into Ray's room and closed the door behind her. Ray's face was all scared, and she didn't want to see it. She examined the evidence instead: a stain like a map in the middle of his soaked sheet. No chance at all for a cover-up, Ivy concluded.

"What'll we do?" Ray said.

"Let's get outa here," she answered. She led him out into the kitchen, and when Sissy turned around Ivy told her, "We're not hungry."

"Not hungry?" Sissy said, instantly alarmed. "Are y'all sick?"

"We're not sick," Ivy said. "We're just not *hungry*, not a bit." She directed Ray toward the door. "So we're gonna skip breakfast today," she said casually, as if they did that from time to time. "Bye," she said, and they were out.

"Are we running away?" Ray said, trotting along beside her.

Ivy didn't think so. "Not exactly," she said. "Not yet."

She knew from her father that it took time to come up with a foolproof getaway. Besides, the moon was getting fuller every night; it was almost time for their midnight race. "We're just taking a little break," she said, and they went on down to their hideout.

They stayed inside the rhododendron for what seemed like hours. They had an extra-long meeting, reviewed the contents of their evidence box, charted the progress of the moon. Finally, though, they got hungry. And hot. And tired of sitting cross-legged under the branches. They decided to go down to the garden and practice for the race, but via the kitchen—where they could sneak some food first.

"What about Marietta?" Ray said, and his stomach growled.

"Oh, what's she gonna do?" Ivy said. "*Kill* us?"— and as soon as she saw Ray's face she was sorry she'd asked. "C'mon," she said, "Marietta's probably not even there. She's probably off committing crimes."

When they emerged from the hideout the bright sun made them blink.

"Someone's here," Ray said, pointing up the driveway to a white van parked beneath the portico.

They approached cautiously, until finally Ivy was

close enough to read the fancy lettering on the side of the truck: HIGH AND DRY PROFESSIONALS. There was a picture of a little man running fast, with cartoon lines coming out of his feet. *Your Moisture-Detection Specialists*, it said.

"Marietta must have leaks," Ivy said. "C'mon," and they went around to the back door. They tiptoed into the kitchen and over to the refrigerator and were reaching into the drawer, for oranges, when they heard Marietta's quavery voice: "Well, *here* you are!"

Ray and Ivy froze, orange-handed. They dropped the fruit and turned to face her. She was standing on the threshold of Ray's room.

"Children," she said, "where *have* you been?"

Ivy couldn't stand the way she was talking to them— as if she cared—or the awful smile she was wearing.

"I want you to come and meet the man from High and Dry." She stepped aside to reveal a stocky man in uniform standing behind her. The name sewn on his pocket said JOHN.

Ivy and Ray walked slowly toward them. Ivy's feet stopped moving before she reached the door, but Marietta drew her forward and ushered her and Ray into Ray's room, next to his bed, which had been stripped bare. On his desk chair, Ivy saw a silver suitcase emblazoned with the High and Dry logo.

"Clearly I needed to take matters into my own hands," she told them. "To nip things in the bud." Ivy didn't like the thought of Marietta nipping. "To finally put an *end* to these *accidents*." She hissed the word. "So I rang up some professionals, and you're just in time for the demonstration," she told them.

John from High and Dry began with a shrug. "It's pretty simple," he said. "Your basic system," and he unsnapped the suitcase and lifted the top. It was packed with some sort of contraption and little gizmos tucked neatly along its sides. He pulled out and unfolded a rubbery sheet that had ripples like fat worms running through it. "This goes on your mattress, see," he said, and he spread it over the mattress and then placed a pad on top of that. He had thick, stubby fingers and moved fast.

Then he lifted out a small black box and plugged it in and set it on the table next to Ray's bed. "At the first sign of moisture," he said, producing a little vial of water from the side of the suitcase and unscrewing its lid, "you get a little wake-up call." He poured a small amount of the water onto the pad, and the box he had

placed on Ray's table exploded in sound. Ivy and Ray jumped. It was like a fire alarm, Ivy thought.

"And at the sound of the bell, you're up and running to the terlet," John said loudly, just to be heard.

Ivy pictured the little cartoon man on the side of the truck, black lines shooting out of his feet. Did he say *terlet*?

John from High and Dry leaned over and shut off the alarm. He opened his thick hands out to them and said, "That's all there is to it." Ray and Ivy stood silent and speechless, staring at the contraption.

Then Marietta's voice came sailing over them. "It's fine, it's fine," she sang out. "It will do *quite* nicely."

John was already snapping his silver suitcase closed, set to be on his way. He grabbed the case by its handle and followed Marietta from the room. "Hey, good luck," he told Ray and Ivy over his shoulder, and Ivy thought how they sure could use some.

Standing beside her brother, face to face with the wired sheet and the pad and the little black box, Ivy waited for a good idea to pop into her head. Nothing popped.

"But where'm I gonna *sleep*?" Ray said.

Ivy turned and looked at him. Her heart sank. She

looked back to the contraption.

"Not on *that*!" Ray said suddenly, horrified.

"C'mon," Ivy said. She knew it was time for another getaway, and she led the way upstairs, to her room.

"Are we running away *now*?" Ray asked hopefully.

It was a close call. Ivy could feel the possibility rising up in her. But they weren't really ready. They had no place to *go*. And they hadn't gotten Marietta yet. And the moon was so close to full! "*Soon*," she said.

Once they were sitting on Ivy's bed, Ray had other questions. "Do you think it *hurts* when it goes off?" he asked. "Do you think you get a shock? Do you think the zapper could *kill* someone?"

"No," she said, and then "*No*" again—this time with greater authority. But his question gave her a good idea. "Hey!" she said. "We can charge Marietta with attempted murder!"

"We can?" Ray said weakly.

"Attempted murder is a really big crime," Ivy went on. "Way bigger than embezzlement. They'll throw the *book* at her! Put her in jail and throw away the key!" Ivy continued, triumphant. "This is great," she finished.

"I don't see what's so great about it," Ray said.

"It's a whole new charge," Ivy said. "A big one."

Ray didn't say anything for a second. "Then can the zapper be evidence?" he asked.

"Yeah," she said. "Definitely. It's kind of like a weapon."

"So can we take it off my bed and store it in the hideout?" Ray said.

"Good idea," she said.

"Can we do it right now?" he wanted to know.

"Why not?" Ivy said. She was excited to be back on Marietta's case— gathering evidence, collecting charges. Plus Ray *wanted* the contraption off his bed. Who wouldn't?

They went back downstairs and pulled it off the mattress and made up the bed without it. Ivy smuggled the sheet outdoors under her shirt, folded up and rubbery and bumpy against her chest. Once they were in the hideout she kind of wrapped it around their shoebox of evidence.

"'T'sugly," Ray said, looking at it.

"Yeah," Ivy agreed. "It is." They studied it in silence a moment more. Then Ivy leaned in closer to Ray with consolation: "But we win."

He shrugged, nodded. He didn't care about winning as much as Ivy. He had another question. "How much longer," he asked, "before twenty-five years is up?"

"Close," Ivy told him. "Close."

The Great Escape

That night, the moon rose round and full in a cloudless sky, right outside Ray's and Ivy's windows. Ivy gasped when she saw it. Even though she had been watching and waiting, night after night, once the real thing was before her—perfect and huge—she could hardly believe her eyes. Everything else paled in the face of it: Marietta, the zapper, comprehensive testing. All Ivy could see was the midnight moonlight adventure that lay ahead of them.

She hurried to get the notes she and Ray had prepared in advance, and she sent her first one down to him: *Tonite is the nite*, signed with the eye. Ray received it, counted to a thousand—a rule they had made—and sent up his reply: a check mark, with the sign of the sun beside it. They settled into their back-and-forth rhythm of sending messages, and the moon sat in the sky, fat and full, like a well-kept promise.

But they had a long way to go until midnight, and after a while Ivy grew a little sleepy and a little chilly sitting by the window, and she occasionally slipped into bed, under her sheets and light blanket, until she heard Ray's whistle and the lovely jingle of charms traveling up the side of the house, signaling another message. She knew Ray did the same. A good bit of time passed between some of their notes.

Suddenly Ivy found herself sitting bolt upright in her bed. Some sound had come into her and brought her back from the little dance she'd been dancing with sleep—not quite dreaming, but not completely awake, either. What was it? Not thunder, not a chiming clock, not an owl, who-ing. Not Ray's alarm!—she had that awful thought before she remembered that they had disconnected and hidden it away; he was safe. She scooted out of bed and went to her window. The moon was still there, same as ever, unchanged. There was no message coming up to her. Everything down below seemed quiet. Everything everywhere seemed quiet.

Something had called her back from sleep, but whatever it was had come and gone. She had no doubt at all that it was midnight.

She retrieved the prize note she had written out, the last one to be sent before the race began—*The Final Owr. Meet by the dor*—and folded it into the pouch and sent it down to Ray. The jewelry jingled, but she had to whistle a long time, too, before he finally came to his window.

After that, they both knew what to do. They had practiced many times, and they were ready.

Ivy slipped on the shorts and shirt that lay folded and waiting on her suitcase stand. She walked to her bedroom door and then stepped out into the hallway. It was dark, and silent. A lone nightlight halfway down cast a dim tunnel of illumination, just enough to highlight the edges of the hanging portraits. Thirty-eight steps, she knew, to get to the back stairway.

She extended her arm so that the tip of her finger just touched the wall, and then she started walking and counting. All the afternoons that she and Ray had practiced this part she had closed her eyes, because she knew that when the time came she would be doing it in the dark. Now she closed her eyes again, partly out of habit and partly so the darkness could seem like a choice. She *wasn't* scared of the dark, she reminded herself. She had been when she was little, but she wasn't anymore. Seventeen. Eighteen. Nineteen. She was using her biggest, most stretched-out steps. Her finger occasionally ran up against the raised frame of a portrait, and then across the bumpy surface of the brushstrokes (Ivy pictured Mustache Man for a moment, but then banished the image), and then up and over the other side of the frame, and back to the wall.

Twenty-nine. Thirty. Almost there. Only the sounds of her own steps. Her finger hit the side of a frame, and then silk cloth—the covered portrait, she knew; a face like Dan's. Keep going, she told herself, keep going. Thirty-seven. Thirty-eight.

She opened her eyes and turned to the right. The staircase was just a few feet ahead of her. She had done a good job counting off. She shot across to it and started down. On the first step she whispered, "Ray, it's me," just like they had planned, so he'd know she was coming. "It's me," she said, on every step. The wooden steps creaked as Ivy descended. She didn't worry, though—Lionel and Marietta were far away in their wing of the house, and now she was so close! One step away! She landed.

"Ivy!" Ray said. He was standing just where they

had planned for him to be: against the refrigerator, right in front of her.

They reached out and grabbed each other's hands and shook them up and down, excitement coursing like electricity through them. They stepped out in front of the refrigerator and Ray pulled open the door. Light sprang into the dark kitchen as they reached for the bags they had hidden at the back of the second shelf, behind all the fancy pre-serves and relishes. They had put them there days ago, in preparation, and each bag contained exactly the same things—a tiny shot glass filched from Lionel's collection in the bar in the library, a little bottle of water into which they had squeezed twenty drops of lemon juice; two

hard candies from the silver dish in the downstairs bathroom; and a banana.

They peeked inside just to make sure the provisions were as they had left them, and then they looked at each other, standing inside the refrigerator's cone of light. Ivy saw Ray: her brother who looked like her, her partner, her best friend in the world. When he turned to close the refrigerator door, she saw his back.

She led the way to the kitchen door, felt for and quietly slid back the bolt that locked it, and turned the knob. She pushed the screen door open and she and Ray stepped out into their perfect night, free.

The moonlight was soft and covered everything like a beautiful veil. It made for a whole new world. Ray and Ivy trotted across the rolling lawn, the grass cool and tickly against their bare feet, and left the big house behind them, dark and quiet and unsuspecting. When they came to the gardens, it was as if they had never really seen them before. The wisteria and vines braided around and dripped from the pergola, but they seem weightier, somehow, and the paths that ran through the rose and herb gardens stood out, mazelike and magical. White flowers sat on their stems as if they were sitting on the night itself. Ray and Ivy quivered with excitement in the cool summer air.

They spread out the contents of their bags on the wooden bench just to the side of the roses, and then they poured a thimbleful of lemon water into their shot glasses. They raised their drinks, clinked them in a toast, and swallowed in a gulp. Ivy had a sudden and deep pang of missing her father. They set down their glasses, and Ivy blew on the back of Ray's neck and he blew on the back of hers—what they always did before big races to give each other power and luck.

Then they went to their starting places: Ivy underneath the pergola, and Ray in the corner by the sunflowers. Even their voices sounded different in the moonlight: more like a song, as they called out in unison, "On your mark, get set...go!" And they were off: on the route they had mapped out and practiced so many times, running, hopping (first on one foot, then on two), skipping, walking fast, walking backwards, back to running, all along the paths of the garden, under the pergola, beside the flowers. Anyone watching them from above would have thought Ray and Ivy had made up a dance, an elaborate garden dance.

Although they had practiced the race many times, they had never before done it in the middle of the night, or by moonlight, and that made all the difference. Ivy could feel it in her bones: she was faster and lighter than she had ever been. She practically leapt as she ran; some internal engine propelled her as she skipped. And Ray was just the same! They had designed the race so that they never once lost sight of each other, and Ivy was aware of him flowing from one part to the next, remembering every move and turn and change in motion, just as they had practiced, shooting along his own route. They had come to the very last part—an all-out run to the top of the ridge that looked down to the river—and they were in perfect step with one another. Charging up to the crest, they arrived at exactly the same moment, arms over their heads in jubilation. Then they bent over, panting, their chests

heaving. Finally, when their breathing was normal, they straightened up, turned to each other, and bowed. It had been a perfect race. They had run it in the moonlight, at midnight, and they had tied.

They bowed again, although that had not been planned, and then they walked back over to the bench and took their places amid the spread-out provisions. They each poured another tiny glass of water and drank. Nothing had ever tasted so good. Then they peeled their bananas, and ate. They leaned back and looked up at the sky.

"Hey, Ivy," Ray said. "What's that light?"

"The moon," Ivy answered, sure without even looking.

But Ray was talking about a football of light, beaming out through a stand of trees. "No," he said. "Look."

Ivy lowered her sights and saw what he meant. "It's the garage," she said. "Veddy must be up." She shivered then, wondering if he spied on them.

Ray asked, "Are you sure he's an accomplice?"

"Pretty," Ivy answered.

"I kinda like him," Ray said.

"You like the limo," Ivy said.

"But I like him, too," Ray said.

"So—you can like an accomplice," Ivy said. She thought of Carol suddenly, and how much she liked *her*.

"Oh," Ray said.

They'd gone back to looking at the moon.

"Wanna race again?" Ivy said, and Ray instantly agreed.

They stuffed their glasses and the banana peels back in their bags, and then they took their places for a rerun of the race.

"On your mark," they sang out. "Get set. Go!" Once again they moved through all the various parts of their race, not quite as fast or as light as the first time—that would have been impossible—but pleasantly, like a happy memory, once again ending in a perfect tie.

And when their second running of the race was finished, so were they—tired and spent and ready to gather their things and walk back up to the big house. They made their way across the lawn, in the moonlight. The light over the garage had gone out.

They crept back inside the house the way they had sneaked outside—locking up what they had unlocked—and stuffed their bags in the trash. Then Ray took his place by the refrigerator and Ivy began her climb to the second floor. Ray would count to fifty and then go to his room—they had agreed it was only fair for him to wait until she made it to her room. Ivy creaked from step to step, made it to the landing, and began the thirty-eight paces back to her doorway. She marched past the covered portrait of Blackstone Mouton Eye Eye Eye and counted down the remaining steps to her bedroom door. When she got to her room she sent off the final note of the night via their intercom: *We are the Best.*

Ray reeled it in, and then they left their windows and climbed into their beds and went to sleep, triumphant.

Caught

When Ivy awoke the next morning, the memory of the race was still pulsing inside her. She hopped out of bed already dressed—she had slept in her shorts and T-shirt—and without a thought trotted downstairs to remember it along with Ray. Retracing the exact route she had taken the night before, she made her way into the kitchen, then tiptoed into Ray's room and stood before him. And when he woke up and saw her standing there, Ivy got to see the race come back to him, too—written all over his face. No one and nothing could ever take it away from them.

The two of them practically strutted into breakfast. Ivy swung her feet as much as she wanted to, heaped her plate with bacon, made faces across the table at Ray, who was only grinning. When Sissy—sad eyes, sad face—entered with the tray, Ivy almost told her to cheer up: things weren't so bad at the big house.

Then, just as Ivy and Ray were preparing to dig in to their breakfast, Marietta announced that the testers from Broken Sparrow Academy would be arriving later that morning.

Ivy ground her teeth and a little growl escaped her. Even sitting across from Ray, she could feel something drop inside him.

Marietta told them to stay close and stay clean after the meal. "I'd hate for you to reflect badly," she said.

What did she think they were? Ivy wondered. Mirrors?

"You children are fortunate," Marietta went on, "to even be *considered* by Broken Sparrow." She handed them a brochure to look at. "See for yourself," she said. "It's the crème de la crème."

After breakfast, Ivy and Ray went upstairs and sat on Ivy's bed. The race was missing from Ray's face, as if the moon had never gotten full.

"The tests won't be so bad," Ivy said. "And then they'll be over."

Ray didn't say a word. He was studying the pictures in the brochure Marietta had given them. "Broken Sparrow is just another big house," he said.

Ivy looked at the colored shots of a mansion set on a hill. "It is," she had to agree. Not all the cream in the world could change that.

At ten o'clock on the dot, a black car—no writing or pictures on the doors—pulled up under the portico. Ivy watched from her window as the testers, a man and a woman, stepped out. Ivy thought they looked like people who went from door to door with Bibles when they weren't testing kids. The woman reminded Ivy of a nun she had seen in an airport once, with a shiny black skirt and a white shirt.

Sissy came upstairs to fetch them, nervous as ever, as if she had to take the tests herself.

"C'mon," Ivy said to Ray, "let's just get it over with," and they followed her down the stairs to where Marietta and the testers were waiting.

Ray got tested in the dining room, and Ivy got tested in the library. The woman provided her with a sharpened pencil and a booklet whose pages were sealed with a small white circle sticker folded over the center.

Ivy sighed: a dot test. She had taken them before, knew all about filling in dots next to the answers she hoped were right. The only parts she really liked were breaking the seal with the end of her #2 pencil, and when the teacher said "Pencils *down*" and it was over.

Ray wasn't old enough for dot tests. The whole time Ivy was taking her test, she could hear the low rumble of voices coming from the dining room, and she knew Ray was working with puzzles and flash cards and getting to say his answers in words. Whatever they were doing sounded better to Ivy than what she was doing, and much easier. It wasn't really fair, she thought, and she would have been mad if she hadn't known that Ray was completely miserable, too.

She was right about the tests not lasting forever, though. They were done before lunch. Then they had to stand in the hallway while Marietta warbled questions to the man and woman about the earliest possible date she could pack the children off to the academy. "The children are *anxious* to begin," she lied as she walked with the testers onto the porch. She called back to Ray and Ivy, "Children, come and say goodbye. And thank you."

Why did *they* have to say thank you? Ivy wondered. They'd had to *take* the tests! But she led Ray outside to mumble some gratitude, and then they stood next to Marietta and waved goodbye (and good riddance). As the man and woman drove off in their black car, Ivy drew her first deep breath of the beautiful day.

Marietta turned to go back in, and Ray and Ivy were just about to take off when Marietta's hands, like claws, landed on each of their shoulders, stopping them cold. "*What* in the name of heaven am I looking at?" she quavered.

Ray and Ivy instantly looked up at Marietta, but she was staring elsewhere—and they followed her stare to the side of the house...to the spot between Ray and Ivy's window...to their intercom! Hanging out, exposed, for the whole world to see. Oh! The one and only morning they had forgotten to haul it back in!

"Nothing," Ivy yelped. "It's nothing."

Marietta turned an icy stare to Ivy. "Au con-traire,"

she said. "It quite clearly is *some*thing," and she headed over to have a closer look.

Ivy and Ray made pleading faces at each other. Then Ivy was off like a shot after Marietta. "We'll take it down," she called. "We'll give it back."

It was like talking to Sissy about the sheets. Marietta wasn't listening. She had walked over to the base of Ray's window and was looking up at the exposed intercom. The bracelet was glorious in the sunlight, sparkling and glinting. The pouch hung from its rawhide string, a sad little sack, empty.

Marietta stood and studied the contraption in silence, mouth slightly agape. "Well, well, well," she said finally. She turned back to the porch. Veddy, who had driven the limo around, was standing there at attention. "Take care of this," she ordered him, and then told Ray and Ivy, "Follow me."

Weighted with dread, they straggled behind her into the big house.

Marietta marched straight into the library, then turned to face them. She didn't say a word but raised her eyebrows up as high as they would go.

"It isn't ours," Ivy tried. The words just popped out.

"Really?" Marietta responded, and her eyebrows went even higher.

Veddy entered then—bracelet and pouch and clothesline in hand.

"Put them on the table," Marietta told him.

The bracelet gave a final little death rattle as he set the pile down.

Now Marietta turned to Ray, leaned in close. "And what do *you* have to say for yourself?" she asked.

Ivy could see Ray's whole body trembling, even his backbone. His shirtsleeve was fluttering.

That's when Ivy cried out. "*I* did it," she said. "I'm the one"—those words popped out of her, too.

Marietta turned from Ray to Ivy. "Is that so?" she said. "Well." She folded her hands together. "I see the acorn doesn't fall far from the tree. You're nothing but a little thief."

"I'm *not* an acorn!" Ivy shot back. "And *you're* a liar!"

Marietta gasped, then pointed her bony finger in Ivy's face. "And you're a little troublemaker," she said. "Do you know what happens to troublemakers? They don't get sent off to fancy boarding schools. Oh, no! They get sent to *reform* school."

A steel door slammed shut in Ivy's mind. Everything went dark gray. *Reform* school?

"Perhaps a year at the Briarpatch School for Wayward Girls is what *you* need," Marietta said. "Let your brother take advantage of Broken Sparrow."

"What?" Ivy croaked. It was getting worse and worse! "You can't send us to *different* schools?" she said. "*Apart!*" A thundering *No!* was rising up inside her, black and huge. But *No* wasn't the word that escaped her mouth. "Kidnapper," she spat.

"Thief!" Marietta's eyes were narrow.

"Attempted murder," Ivy said. "-Er."

"Savage," Marietta hissed.

"Witch!"

They stopped then, eyes locked, chins thrust forward, fists clenched.

"Witch!" Ivy declared again, for good measure, and stamped her foot.

A moment of pure silence followed, and then Marietta did a truly scary thing: she smiled. "So I'm a witch, am I?" she said, leaning in even closer to Ivy. "*That's* what you think? And I suppose you think I have you under my evil spell?" She wiggled her bony fingers in the air as if she were doing magic. "You and little what's-his-name? Well, perhaps I have. And perhaps from now on you'll mind your p's and q's—if you *know* what's good for you," Marietta said.

Ivy knew that Ray and her sticking together was good. And Carol and Dan. She didn't breathe a word of it.

"And if you *do* know what's good for you, you'll tell me right here and now every little thing you two have been up to. What other mischief? What *else* have you stolen?"

Ivy clamped her mouth tight and then tighter. She'd never confess. But suddenly a flood of words—a gusher—came pouring out of Ray!

"I'll sleep on the zapper," he blurted. "The crack was an accident, in the glass. We'll give up the hat and the will. And the testament. Don't send Ivy away."

Marietta, clearly surprised by the onslaught of Ray's confession, suddenly raised up her hand like a crossing guard. "Stop," she said. "Did you say *will*?" It was as if a current of electricity had shot through the room—and straight through Marietta.

There was silence. Ivy knew that something big had happened, but she didn't know why or what it was.

"Did you?" Marietta repeated, and Ivy and Ray slowly nodded.

"*Well*, then," Marietta said. All of a sudden her voice was drippy sweet and that awful smile of hers was starting up. "No need to get ourselves all worked up over a few missing items—trinkets, really." She waved at the bracelet, dismissing it the way she dismissed Ray and Ivy from the table. "Simply hand the will over to me and that will be that. We'll forget all about this other unfortunate business."

Ivy stood still, thought hard. How much Marietta

wanted that will was written all over her. Finally she answered. "What'll you give *us*?"

"*Im*pudent child!" Marietta sputtered, straightening up. But then she regained her composure, drew her hands together. "I do believe I've met my match," she said over her shoulder. Veddy was standing straight and still by the door. Marietta studied Ivy. She twisted her held hands. "Fine," she said finally. "*Fine.*" Her voice was like scissors. "So tell me, child—just what *is* it that you want?"

It was a big question—a huge one—and Ivy was unprepared. She didn't know. "One minute," she said, and she grabbed Ray and pulled him away to the farthest corner of the room, as far away from Veddy and Marietta as they could get.

"OK, Ray," Ivy whispered close. "This is it. Our chance. What do we want?"

Ray's eyes got big. "The limo?" he said.

"C'mon, Ray," Ivy urged. "We can do better than that."

Ray thought. "Every wish we want forever?"

"Oh, Ray," Ivy said. "This isn't a fairy tale! This is real! This is Marietta!"

"Well, what do *you* want?" he said.

And as soon as Ray asked her, she knew—for both of them. She knew. Dan and Carol. *Dan and Carol!* What else? Her mother's perfect red curls, Dan's million-dollar smile.

"The clock is ticking, and I *will* have that will," Marietta called over to them.

"OKOK," Ivy answered. She had an idea.

"What do you mean, a trial?" Marietta said when she heard. "A *trial?* What kind of nonsense is this?"

"*We* give you the will," Ivy said, "if *you* stand trial—including a verdict and sentence," she added. She felt like she was playing cards—betting and bluffing and raising the ante all at the same time.

"A *trial?*" Marietta repeated, as if she didn't know what the word even meant. "What on earth...?" she said, and then, "Are you referring to some kind of *game?*" *Game* was another word that sounded dirty when she said it—the same as when she said *play* and *child.*

"Here in the entryway," Ivy declared. "And you have to do what we say. In half an hour. You can bring Lionel. And Sissy. And Veddy," she added. She turned to personally invite him, but he was gone. "I mean

Andrew," she said. She turned back to Marietta. "Take it or leave it," Ivy said. She hoped she had her best poker face on.

"Oh, for heaven's sake," Marietta said. She sighed deeply, as if she were holding on to her last shred of patience with her long, bony fingers. "Very well. I'll indulge you in your little whim. We'll play your silly game of trial. And then you will hand over the will to me." She turned from them and swept out the library door. A moment later she turned back to threaten: "*Or else!*"

The Discovery Phase

Ivy and Ray didn't dawdle. They headed straight down to their hideout to collect the will.

"Are we *really* gonna put Marietta on trial?" Ray was scurrying to keep up with Ivy, asking questions along the way.

"You bet we are," Ivy told him.

"What good is that?" he wanted to know.

"Because then we can find her guilty and sentence her and she *has* to do what we say: that's what a sentence *is*," Ivy told him. Just thinking about it put a little spring in her step. When they reached the opening to their hideout, though, Ivy suddenly veered away and headed up the hill.

"Where are we going?" Ray said.

"They could be watching us," she said. "Staking us out." That happened all the time in movies she watched with Dan. "We can't take any chances," she told Ray. She still wasn't sure about Veddy. She led Ray up the crest of lawn, to their lookout over the river. They stopped there, panting.

The river stretched out before them, sparkling in the sun as if diamonds had been sprinkled across the top of it.

She could see Ray following its trail as far as he could.

"They're closer than ever," she promised him.

He looked at her.

"But you have to go along with me," she said. "This isn't just practice," she told Ray. "This is the real thing. This is *it*!"

"OK," Ray agreed, climbing on board the way he always did.

Ivy surveyed the estate from their perch on the hill and finally declared it safe to sneak back down to their hideout. They didn't see anyone around, lingering, but Ivy stayed outside and stood guard, just in case, while Ray crawled in to get their shoebox of evidence.

He was in there a long time. "Hurry up," she called to him. "We don't have all day."

He finally crawled out, with shoebox in hand, but bad news. "The will's gone," he told her. "It's *gone!*"

"What?" Ivy shrieked.

"But look what I found," he said, and held out a handful of silver-wrapped chocolates.

Ivy scoured the hideout and searched the shoebox herself before she would believe it was missing. "Oh, gimme a chocolate," she finally said to Ray in desperation. She unpeeled it, added the silver to their ball, and popped the chocolate in her mouth. As she sucked on the candy, a plan came into her head.

"Marietta *thinks* we have the will," Ivy said. "She doesn't know we don't. We'll bluff," she decided. She was trying to remember everything Dan had ever taught her about playing poker, especially bluffing. She was

not about to lose their one shot at putting Marietta on trial. "I'll sentence her to not *see* the will," she said. "I'll think of *some*thing."

"But where'd it go?" Ray said.

"Oh, Ray," Ivy said. "It just *went*. Things come and go." She was already practicing her bluffing for Ray's sake, and maybe her own, too, because she was actually very worried about where the will had gone and who might have taken it—so worried, in fact, that she just couldn't think about it. "Hand me another chocolate," she said.

They'd finished off the stash of kisses by the time they made their way back up to the big house, and Ivy had left the unfortunate business of the missing will behind her. Standing in the grand entryway, she was completely transported by how perfect a setting it was for the trial. "It's majestic," she declared—ideal for making people feel small. She also liked how sounds echoed inside it. She would do her judging from one of the top stairs, where she could look out over the whole room, from above.

"What about the crack?" Ray said. "In the glass?"

The memory came crashing back. "We'll put you in

front of it," she told him. "That'll be your position. And we'll put Marietta where she can't see it anyway."

Next they stashed the shoebox and the zapper in the library. "I'll make my entrance from here," Ivy decided. She remembered the judge coming out from his little door in the corner at her parents' trial and what a strong impression it had made on her.

Then she and Ray dragged chairs from the dining room into the entryway and faced them toward the staircase. Ivy set one all on its own, in front of the others. "For Marietta," she said.

"Does she get a lawyer?" Ray asked.

"She doesn't deserve one," Ivy answered, but she had to admit he was right. Everyone gets a lawyer. "Oh, OK," she said, giving in. "She can have Lionel."

"Lionel doesn't talk," Ray said.

"*Fine*," Ivy said. And she dragged another chair up next to Marietta's, for Lionel to sit in and say nothing. "They don't help anyway," she said. Her parents' lawyer hadn't.

"C'mon," she told him. "We need to do the witness stand. It should go here," she said, making an X with her foot on one of the black diamond tiles in the center of the floor. They dragged out the fanciest dining room chair—the one with carved arms—but Ivy said it wouldn't do. Then she got a good idea. "Oh, Ray!" she said. "Lionel's chair. The one that goes up."

They went back to the library to see if they could possibly move it. They pressed the button on the cord until the chair spread out like a bed. Then they pushed and pulled it, off the carpet and over the threshold onto the polished tiles of the entryway. From there they had smooth sailing, straight to the spot Ivy wanted.

But when Ray pressed the button, nothing happened. "We broke it," he said.

Those miserable words!

Then Ivy spied another wire peeking out from under the chair. "It's electric!" she cried. She stretched the wire to the nearest outlet and bent down to plug it in, hesitating for just a moment at the thought of Marietta owning an electric chair. She didn't tell Ray what she was thinking, though; she didn't want to scare him.

She went ahead and plugged it in, and the chair was up and running. But when they turned around they saw that pushing it out had left black skidmarks all across the white diamonds, as if the chair had sped itself out to the center of the room.

"Uh-oh," Ray said.

"Never mind," Ivy said, squinting. "You can hardly see them."

They stood and squinted together.

"Let's get changed," Ivy said. She wanted to be in her robe.

They were halfway up the stairs when they heard a gasp from down below. Sissy had come into the entryway and discovered the black marks all over the floor. When she looked up at Ray and Ivy, end-of-the-world was written all over her face.

"Sissy... ," Ivy called out to her like a dog she wanted not to bark. The last thing she needed right now was a hissy fit from Sissy.

"Just *look* at this mess!" Sissy said, stretching out her skinny arms toward the floor.

Ivy was tripping down the stairs to stand beside her. A picture flashed in Ivy's mind: Sissy on all fours, scrubbing away, crying into her bucket of sudsy water like some miserable rindercella. Ivy saw their majestic trial going up in smoke. "It's OK," she called out, "not a problem, don't worry, we'll fix it." She couldn't reassure fast enough.

"Oh, Mrs. Noland's not going to like this one *tiny* bit," Sissy said. She turned her distraught face toward Ivy.

She was ready to bawl, Ivy could tell, and what came out of Ivy's mouth next was a command: "Sissy!" she said sharply. "*Do* control yourself!"

The effect was instantaneous. Sissy startled as if she'd been hit with cold water, and straightened herself up.

"It's OK," Ivy said again. "We'll take care of all this later. We're going to have a trial and we're just getting set up for it," she told her. And then, because she was feeling a bit frayed herself, Ivy said, "So why don't you just ease up on the Sarah Heartburn?"

"The what?" Sissy said. Her sad face got all confused.

Sarah Heartburn was Dan's name for anyone he considered high-strung. "The crying, the waterworks—they're a little over the top," Ivy told her. She felt she had to let Sissy know.

Sissy's mouth made an O. "Well, *you'd* cry too," she answered back, "if you were trapped in this place with Mrs. Noland, a million miles from home, snatched away from your baby brother..."

"What do you mean?" Ivy said.

"That's right," Sissy said. "Mrs. Noland said that if I worked real hard and minded my p's and q's she'd see about having Luther come and live here too, but she hasn't done a *thing* about it. First there was the trial and then you-all arrived and meanwhile my heart is just about breaking I'm so homesick..."

"Wait a minute!" Ivy said. "Marietta's keeping you apart from your *brother*?" All of a sudden she was seeing Sissy with different eyes, hearing her with different ears.

"She sure is. And Luther

and I are like *this*," Sissy said, raising up two twined fingers to show just exactly how close. "Have been since we were babies," she finished.

"That's terrible," Ivy said. "It's *criminal*!" she declared, and when she said so, everything came rushing back at her: the trial, the charges, the need to get into her robe. "Sissy," she said, "Ray and me'll take care of the skidmarks. We'll make it so you and Luther get back together. We'll fix everything," she promised. "But we have to get Marietta first. So let us have our trial and try not to be such a cry—" *Crybaby* is what she had started to say, but she caught herself. "Just keep it down, OK?"

With her chin still quivering Sissy gave Ivy a shaky nod, and Ivy thumped her on the back for good luck and then raced up the stairs to Ray.

"What—" He started right in with a question, but Ivy cut him off.

"C'mon," she said, "the clock is ticking."

It was time to disrobe the portrait.

This time they were fast and efficient, like old pros, standing on tiptoe on their chairs, swinging the material off the picture in one grand swoop, giving only a backwards glance to EyeEyeEye. Ivy gathered the black material in, clutched it close to her chest.

"Waitaminute," Ray said. "It's my turn."

She froze. "What?"

"My turn," he repeated. "To be judge. 'Member?"

She did remember. But she couldn't stand it. Not now, not for *this* trial! "Ray," she said, instantly begging. She was itching to wrap the black sheet around herself and make a grand entrance. She was all set to call her court to order. And she was dying to hand down the sentence.

But Ray was shaking his head. "No fair," he said, pulling the bundle of material away from her. "It's my turn. You promised."

It was almost more than she could bear, having to let Ray be the judge. Her fists tightened around the material. "Ray," she said. "You can be the *pro*secutor!" She had a sudden memory of watching crime shows on TV with her father—a million of them—and how Dan always knew, in advance, how they'd turn out.

"What is it?" Ray asked, wary. "Prosecutor."

"The guy who proves you're guilty," Ivy said.

"I didn't do anything," Ray protested.

"Not *you*, Ray—*Marietta*! You can ask a ton of questions," she said, to tempt him. "Anything you want to know. You *love* questions, Ray. And you can ask the same question over and over. We *need* you to ask the questions. You're the *king* of questions." She could see him wavering. "C'mon, Ray," she urged him. "Pleeeze. I'll give you the next *eleven* turns!"

Ray's grip on the material loosened. "O...K," he agreed, reluctantly, and took a step back. He always gave in to her. It was one of the things Ivy loved most about him.

They made their final preparations in the library. Ivy was robed; Ray had on his Bruins jacket. Ivy was kneeling over their box of evidence, intently examining each piece. She had everything spread out: the picture from the paper, the top hat, their ball of silver foil, their drawings of the moon, the marriage certificate, the zapper...

Evidence still didn't interest Ray the way it did Ivy; he was looking through the desk drawers.

"Maybe we should show the black box, too. Set off the alarm," Ivy said, considering.

"Hey, look," Ray said.

"Save the zapper for last," Ivy advised. "It's our best exhibit."

"Look, Ivy," Ray said.

"Or you could show it *first*," Ivy said, on second thought.

Bam!

Ivy wheeled around to a grinning Ray, brandishing a small brown hammer in his hand. She flew across the room and was holding it in a flash. It was made of wood, with a skinny, grooved handle and a top that was more like a spool. Engraved on the side of the spool,

in tiny letters, was *Lionel Noland, Class of '39.* Ray had found it in the top desk drawer.

Ivy tapped gently on a coaster filled with people on horses chasing a fox. The hammer fit perfectly in her hand; it felt and sounded just right. "Oh, Ray," Ivy said. "You are the *best!*" She even felt a fleeting fondness for Lionel.

Suddenly they heard Marietta, warbling: "Children? Where are you? I haven't got all day!"

Ray and Ivy blew down each other's backs for power and luck one last time. "Wait till everyone's here," Ivy told him, "and then announce 'All rise.'" She opened the door and Ray slipped out.

Finally Ivy was alone—in the library, fully robed, hammered. She was surrounded by books. She got nervous waiting for her entrance call and began to pace around and around the perimeter of the room, dragging her index finger along the backs of the books—a steady *bump, bump, bump* along the fat and thin spines, the cloth or leather or paper. It calmed her, going around in circles.

At the end of one of her rounds, she spied a book she had seen their very first night at the big house: *Crime and Punishment.* She pulled it off the shelf and held the weighty volume in both her hands. It was way too heavy to throw at anyone, but it gave her a good idea.

She cracked the door and whispered, "Hey, Ray." He trotted right over to her, and she handed him the book and told him to use it to swear in witnesses. And then, because she couldn't help it, she offered a few last tips on how to be a prosecutor. "Say 'and' before your questions," she told him, "and talk like you know they're lying." She demonstrated: "'And *what* is your name? And how *long* have you been a witch?' See?"

Ray nodded. The book was heavy for him to hold.

"And you can walk back and forth with your hands behind your back. And rub your chin like you're pulling on your beard." Ivy could tell he wasn't really listening. "Oh, never mind," she said finally. "Just ask whatever you want and then I'll sentence her."

The Trial

"All rrrrrise!" Ray sang out, and the trial of Ivy's dreams began.

She made her entrance with a flourish of material she had left undraped for just that purpose. Ray was positioned in front of the cake, and he was grinning, but she managed not to grin back. She lifted her head a notch higher, serious as could be, and proceeded toward the staircase.

She had wrapped the robe close around her ankles, and mounting the stairs was a tricky proposition, but she took her time and told herself that slowness added dignity. When she reached the eleventh step, Ivy stopped, turned, and looked out over her courtroom. There was Marietta, below her—just where she belonged, Ivy thought. Her dress had clusters of ugly purple grapes printed on it. Lionel was standing—barely—beside her, and Veddy, in full uniform, had positioned himself behind them. Sissy, wide-eyed and pale, held herself in a tight crisscross of arms that Ivy took as an obvious effort at control.

Ivy drew a deep breath, then raised her right hand and brought down the little hammer against the fox-chasing coaster in her left. What a pure, clear sound it made—straight up her backbone, right out the top of her head: the sound she'd been dying to make. "This court is in order," she called out, so thrilled she almost forgot to name Marietta as the defendant, or charge her with the crime. "Attempted murder," she called out finally, when she came to her senses. Then she told everyone to sit down, and sat down herself, and nodded at Ray to begin.

He reconfirmed with Ivy: "I get to ask anything?"

"Anything," she answered.

"Marietta first," he called out, and motioned for her to come to the witness stand. He held out *Crime and Punishment,* and Marietta put her bony hand on it and promised to tell the whole truth and nothing but it.

"Ha!" Ivy said, from up above.

Marietta shot her a withering look.

Ray had set down *Crime and Punishment* and picked up the cord that raised and lowered Lionel's chair. "Go ahead," he told Marietta, "sit down," and when she had seated herself, he pressed on the button and the back of the chair began to lower.

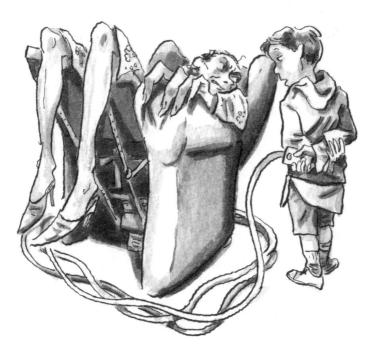

Ivy thought of the one time in her life she'd been to the dentist, and felt glad she wasn't sitting where Marietta was right now.

Ray didn't lower Marietta very far before he started in with his questions. "How *old* are you?" he began.

She clucked her tongue and said that polite children didn't ask such things.

Ivy pounded her little hammer. Oh, that sweet, pure sound! "Overruled," she called out, and tapped the coaster again. She was going to overrule everything!

She told Marietta to answer the question.

"Seventy-seven," Marietta sniffed. "If you must know."

"Lucky numbers," Ray responded. Then he clasped his hands behind his back and paced around the recliner.

Ray's a natural, Ivy thought from above.

"And what's that thing you cut off the top of your egg with?" he asked Marietta next. He paused and stroked his chin. *"And where'd you get it?"* His voice was strong. He looked good. *"And why didn't you just* eat *the wedding cake? And didn't it ever rain in Spain when* you *were a kid?"* He rolled out question after question. *"And how come you covered that picture in the hall with a black sheet?"*

Marietta jolted a bit at his question about the portrait. "I beg your pardon," she said.

"That guy," Ray said. "Blackstone Mouton EyeEye -Eye. How come he got covered up?"

Marietta choked a little. "Whatever are you talking about?" she said. She tried to sit forward, but the chair wouldn't really let her.

"The guy with the hat under the sheet," Ray persisted. "Who looks like Dan."

"I don't know what you're talking about," Marietta said.

Ivy banged her hammer. "Liar," she called down, just because she could.

Marietta's hand flew to her chest, right over a cluster of grapes.

"Answer the question," Ivy said.

"Some dumb relative?" Ray suggested—what Ivy had told him. He was only trying to help.

Marietta was indignant. "Hardly," she said. "Blackstone had a *brilliant* mind—criminal though it was," she added, almost under her breath. She once again tried to straighten up. "If you must know," she said, "he's the only son of Blackstone Mouton the Second," she said. "My dear departed father."

"Your father's son?" Ray repeated.

"Yes."

"You mean—he's your *brother*?" Ivy called down to the witness chair. She didn't mean to butt in on Ray's questions, but she couldn't help herself.

Marietta extended her chin farther into the air. "Yes," she said. "My *late, estranged, disowned* brother."

"He's late?" Ray said.

"Dead," Marietta clarified.

"Is that why you covered him up with a sheet?" Ray asked.

She pinched her lips together; her mouth was a wrinkled line. "Not exactly," she said.

"Why then?" Ray asked. "Exactly."

Marietta folded her hands together in a tight grip. "The portrait was covered shortly after he was expelled from the military academy, and my father turned him out on his own. And it has remained draped these many years—until *now*, I see," she said, glaring up at Ivy in her robe.

Ivy overlooked Marietta's look.

"Your brother got kicked out?" Ray said. "What'd he do?" he asked, deeply interested.

Marietta turned away. "He was impossible. Delinquent. Incorrigible. He squandered every opportunity he was given. My father had no *choice* but to disown him, to protect the good name of our family."

"Disown?" Ray said.

"Cut out, cut off, expel," Marietta answered.

"Wait a minute," Ivy called down. "You kicked your brother out of your *family*?" she asked.

A sudden strangled cry erupted from Sissy, who was sagging in her chair.

"That's *bad*," Ray judged.

"This has gone far enough," Marietta declared. She tried to stand up, but the chair was tilted back far enough that her skinny legs only pedaled the air. Her hands grasped at the armrests. "Let me *out* of here!" she demanded.

Ray pressed the button and the chair slowly started to rise.

Marietta was finally able to stand. She straightened herself, patted her hair. "I've played along with your little game, answered your silly questions. Now it's time to hand over the will." She extended her arm up toward Ivy. "Give it to me *now*," she said.

The will blazed in Ivy's mind. They had it—they *didn't* have it! She was bluffing, and her bluff had been called. But before she'd even begun to stammer out an excuse, Veddy was up and out of his seat, stepping forward, waving something in the air as he approached the staircase. The will!

"Hey!" Ivy shouted. "You stole that!"

"As did you," he answered, with a small, elegant bow.

Marietta was rushing over, ready to grab it from him—"Give that to me this *instant*," she demanded—

but Veddy easily held it above her head, out of reach.

"Shall I not be called to testify?" he asked. "Is this or is this not a trial?"

Ivy and Ray looked from Veddy to Marietta and back to each other with big eyes. Then Ivy made the call. She wanted to see what Veddy had up his sleeve. "Swear in the next witness," she ruled.

Marietta, grumbling but resigned, reclaimed her seat next to Lionel.

Ray once again hoisted up the big, fat *Crime and Punishment*. Veddy placed his hand on it and promised to tell the truth. "Unlike *others* who have gone before me," he added, at the end.

Before he sat down, Veddy extended his hand to Ray, for the control that operated the chair. "*I'll* drive," he said, and Ray turned it over. Veddy seated himself, stretched out at a comfortable but dignified angle, and then told Ray to begin, he was ready.

Ray checked again with Ivy: "Anything?"

"Anything," she told him. "But ask about the will."

"How come you took it?" Ray began. "The will?"

"Ah, yes," Veddy answered. "The will. Why, to see what it said! So kind of you, by the way, to finally locate it. We'd looked all over for it, you know—combed every nook and cranny of this blasted place."

"For what?" Ray said. "What is it? What difference does it make?"

"Ah," Veddy said, "a significant difference. Without a will the estate was due to be divided among *all* the surviving relatives of Blackstone Mouton the Second."

Marietta was on her feet, hissing at Veddy. "Silence. I demand you be quiet!"

Ivy pounded her hammer with vigor. "Order in the court," she cried out. "Or I'll have you removed!" She hammered once more, because she could.

Marietta sat down. Veddy went on.

"As I was saying," he said. "With no will on record, Mrs. Noland was most anxious to position herself as the sole eligible heir."

"Because she didn't want to share?" Ray said.

"Precisely," Veddy said. "Well put. She wanted all the other relatives out of the picture."

"Who else is there?" Ray said. "I thought that guy was late and got disowned. Plus he died."

"Ah yes, Master Blackstone and his sad demise. In San Quentin, I believe it was—am I correct in that, Mrs. Noland?" He turned to look at Marietta, whose face was pulsing purple. Then he addressed Ray directly: "Perhaps you children know him by his other name, Blackie Mutton?"

Ray and Ivy responded in unison, as if they were calling a race: "Blackie Mutton?" they repeated. "*Grampa* Blackie?" Their famous grandfather who had pulled off one of the biggest bank robberies in the history of California?

"Grampa Blackie Mutton...is Blackstone Mouton EyeEyeEye?" Ivy said.

"One and the same," Veddy said. "I believe you noted a family resemblance," he said to Ray.

"He looks like Dan!" Ray said.

"Only fitting," Veddy answered. "Since he *was* your father's father. As well as Marietta's brother," he added.

Once again Marietta was on her feet, objecting. "Don't listen to a word this man says," she sputtered. "He's a traitor and a criminal."

Even Lionel was sitting up, wide awake.

Ray was confused. He called up to Ivy, "*Who's* related?"

"Everyone," Ivy answered him. That's what it sounded like to her.

"Are *we*?" he asked. "Related to Marietta?"

It was a gruesome thought. But if Grampa Blackie was her brother, didn't they have to be? "Order in the court," she called out, for no reason, and hammered.

"What is she?" Ray asked. "To us?"

A witch, Ivy thought. A kidnapper. An attempted murderer. But she knew what Ray meant. "Family," she had to answer. "An aunt, maybe?"

"An ant?" Ray repeated.

"An awwnt."

"Your *great* aunt," Marietta suddenly corrected.

"She only *thinks* she's great," Ivy said to Ray. They both turned and looked at her. She was seated, and fuming, and glaring.

"What about Lionel?" Ray asked.

"An in-law," Veddy answered.

"And Grampa Blackie?"

"An outlaw," Veddy answered.

"Why didn't he ever tell where he came from?" Ray asked.

"Oh, Ray," Ivy called down. "Think if Marietta was *your* sister—wouldn't *you* wanna keep it secret?"

"I *beg* your pardon," Marietta called out.

"Are we related to *you*?" Ray asked Veddy, hopefully.

"Absolutely not," Veddy said. "I'm deeply relieved to say that I don't have a drop of this family's blood in me, though I've spent thirty-two years of my life in its employ—first for Blackstone Mouton the Second and most recently for Mrs. Noland."

"Whose accomplice *are* you, anyway?" Ivy called down. He sure didn't seem on Marietta's side anymore.

"I serve whichever master employs me," he answered.

"And you'll be employed not a minute more if you don't turn over that will," Marietta threatened.

"Ah, the will," Veddy said. "Yes, I imagine you're wondering what it says, aren't you?"

There was silence.

"Apparently Mr. Mouton came to the conclusion, late in life, that if there was any hope to be found it lay with *future* generations," Veddy said. "Thus his instruction to create the Last, Best Hope Charity."

"And I *did* that!" Marietta cried out. "I welcomed these little ragamuffins into my home, offered them their first taste of refinement..."

Ivy assumed she was talking about bacon, which Ivy had actually eaten precious little of.

"And from the beginning I did what he asked: I set up the charity, filed the required papers..." Marietta had raised her hand and was shaking her bony finger.

Veddy icily observed her. "So you did," he said. "And then recruited a known embezzler to run it!"

Ivy was sensitive to the word *embezzler* (and its relatives: *embezzlement, embezzling*). "Wait a minute!" she cried out. "You *brought* Dan here to embezzle from the charity? I thought you wanted all the money for yourself!"

Veddy answered for Marietta. "Mrs. Noland had your family under surveillance for years," he said. "She was not unaware of your father's, ah, expertise with numbers, or his brushes with the law. She felt confident that, given the chance to run a charity, he would do what came naturally to him. And when he did, she had the perfect excuse for taking it over herself and sending him away."

"Up the river," Ray contributed.

"Indeed," Veddy said. "And ineligible to claim any inheritance even if he were to discover his family line. Once he was gone, all that remained was getting you children out of the picture."

"What picture?" Ray asked.

"Not a pretty one," Veddy answered.

Fresh outrage was surging in Ivy. "You *tricked* Dan!" she cried. "That's no fair. That's a sting!" she blurted, pointing at Marietta. She knew from movies. She knew from Dan. "You set him up," she said. "That's a crime!"

"Precisely," Veddy concurred, "which is a *most* unfortunate development for Mrs. Noland, given a very important stipulation in Blackstone Mouton's will..."

Everyone turned to him, watched and waited to hear what he would tell them next.

"Mr. Mouton was quite adamant that his estate be divided among only those relatives untouched by criminal activity." He turned to Marietta. " —A status to which you might have laid claim prior to this nasty business with the charity and the entrapment and the perjury, but which eludes you now, I'm afraid. I believe you've joined all the family criminals who have gone before you—if not up the river, then most certainly out in the cold. Which leaves only the great-grandchildren in line to inherit the estate."

Marietta's fists tightened on her bony knees.

"What?" Ray said. "Who gets what?"

"His great-grandchildren," Veddy said. "Every-thing." He looked from Ray to Ivy. "*You two* are the greats," he finished.

"We are?" Ray asked.

"We are!" Ivy cheered.

"Indeed," Veddy said.

"You're fired," a broken Marietta quavered out to Veddy.

"You're hired," Ivy countered. She definitely wanted Veddy on her side.

"At your service," he said, with a little bow from deep within the witness seat.

"I've had quite enough of this," Marietta said, rising a little shakily from her chair in front. "Enough of this silly game."

Ivy brought down her hammer. "*I* say when court

is over," she insisted. She paused, then brought down her hammer again. "And I say it's over," she said. "I mean recessed," she amended. They hadn't even exhibited the zapper, but she had found out plenty. She had found out more than she'd ever dreamed of knowing.

The Sentence

Ray, Ivy, and Veddy clustered near the witness chair. Marietta and Lionel limped upstairs to rest. Sissy plastered herself against the wall near the library.

Clicking his heels, Veddy announced himself at Ray and Ivy's service.

"So you're definitely on *our* side now, right?" Ray reaffirmed.

"I make it a point to *always* be on the winning side," Veddy told them.

"Then let's take a spin in the limo," Ray suggested.

"I can't," Ivy said. "I have to deliberate."

"I thought you said it was recess."

"It is...I did," Ivy admitted. "But I have to think," she told him.

"About what?" Ray said.

"This is a complicated case, Ray," Ivy said. Her head was still spinning with questions and answers. She turned to Veddy suddenly. "Why didn't old Moneybags just give it all to Marietta?" she asked him.

He chuckled. "Couldn't *stand* the old gal," he said. "Couldn't stand her! It's surely why he hid his will—just to torment her."

"Hide-and-seek," Ray said.

"A *game*," Ivy said, in perfect imitation of Marietta's disgust.

Then Ray asked about the only thing still bothering him. "Why would Marietta's father kick someone out of his own *family*?" he said. "Wouldn't he feel bad?"

"Maybe that's why he left us the money," Ivy said. "Even though he didn't know us—to make up for what he did to Blackie. Pay his debt to society," she said. "To pillars like us." She stood up taller.

"Actually," Veddy interjected, "Mr. Mouton was not what you would call a forgiving man, nor was he prone to regret. He was quite prepared to go on punishing

Blackie from beyond the grave—by disinheriting not only Blackie, but *any* of his descendants who, ah, veered from the path."

"Like Dan," Ivy said.

"Precisely."

"Or Marietta," Ivy said. "Now *there's* a criminal."

"Indeed."

"But not us!" Ivy added.

"Not you," Veddy agreed. "You're clean, as they say."

"If we watch our p's and q's," Ivy said, at which point Ray had lost interest in the conversation. He reached out and took Veddy's hand and once again asked for a spin in the limo.

"Go, then," Ivy told them. "Play." She had more thinking to do.

Ivy made a beeline to the library, which she now considered her chambers. Sissy was plunked down in a chair by the door, her arms wrapped around herself—a Pitiful Pearl if ever there was one, Ivy thought.

"Sissy," she said, approaching her. "It's over. We win."

Sissy didn't move, just lifted her sad gray eyes, all teared up, to Ivy.

Ivy sighed. She remembered what Sissy had said about her baby brother Luther, how Marietta had pulled them apart. She gripped the hammer tight in her hand. "You get a raise," she said. "Call your brother and tell him to hop on a bus."

Sissy jolted to attention and burst out crying.

"But use the phone in the kitchen," Ivy suggested. She needed quiet for her deliberations.

Sissy scurried off to make her call, and Ivy finally stepped into the library and closed the door behind her. There, surrounded by books, she was determined to get the story straight in her mind once and for all. She began to pace, making her rounds of the room, running her finger along the backs of the books, going over everything, over and over, round and round:

Marietta *bump* and Blackie Mutton were brother

and sister *bump bump*; Blackstone Mouton was their father *bump bump*, but he kicked out *bump* Blackie from home. Blackie went on *bump* to become a bank robber and never talked *bump* about home. Dan didn't know *bump* and neither did Carol; Marietta surveilled them all. She wanted the money so she *bump* set a trap to get Dan sent away *bump* forever. Ivy and Ray were next on her list, but *bump* they found the will. Where there's a will there's a *bump bump* way. Now Veddy is on their *bump* side. And everything's theirs because they are great, just the two of them, great, *bump bump bump*.

Ivy came to the end of a round. She stopped her

pacing, dropped her hand to her side, let out a sigh of relief. Finally she had what she wanted: all the answers. And she knew what she was going to do.

"All rrrrise," Ray called out.

He had returned from his spin in the limo—his teeth were coated with chocolate—and Ivy had told him to reconvene the court.

Now, right on cue, Ivy opened the library door and stepped into the grand entryway. Her head was high and her mind, as always, made up. She crossed the black and white diamond tiles and made her way to the staircase.

Ray had taken up his position in front of the cake and was grinning like crazy, jiggling his eyebrows at her, squirming as if the best secret in the world were swimming inside him. Ivy wished he would stop it. This was her final entrance! She was just about to mount the first step when he called out in a loud whisper, "Hey Ivy, lookit."

Before she could even shush him he stepped aside, and Ivy instantly saw what he was talking about. She gasped. There was the spider—out of the cake and resting on top of the empty scroll in the wire holder—

and it was even bigger than Ivy remembered.

Now the others—Marietta, Veddy, Sissy, even Lionel—were edging closer to see.

"Oh, *my*!" Marietta cried out when she spotted it.

Lionel lifted his magnifying glass.

Ray started tapping on the dome.

"Don't!" Ivy said.

"It can't get us," Ray told her, and kept tapping.

"*Kill* it," Marietta demanded.

Lionel moved his magnifying glass up close, then far away. He couldn't locate what they were talking about.

Ivy saw Sissy twitching, getting herself all worked up.

Veddy stepped forward. "Allow *me*," he said, and in one fluid motion lifted the side of the dome, reached in, and scooped the spider into his hand. He set down the dome—the side with the crack, Ivy registered, with dread—and extended his closed fist to Ray. "What shall I do with him?" he asked.

Ray gave a little shrug. "I dunno," he said. "Set him free?"

"Veddy good," Veddy answered, and with a few long strides was over to the front door. He was out and back in just a few seconds, brushing his hands one against the other. "As you wished," he said to Ray.

Marietta, meanwhile, had discovered the crack in the glass. "Oh, *my*," she said again, this time more of a lament. "*Everything*'s falling apart!" she cried to the air.

Ivy wanted to change the subject. She didn't like spiders and she certainly didn't want Marietta distracted by the crack. Besides, she had work to do, sentences to give. "Let's take it from the top," she said, clapping her hands. "Everyone back to their seats. Ray, call the court to order, and I'll make my entrance. Again!"

The second time around, things went without a hitch. Ivy solemnly made her way up the stairs and stood tall on the eleventh step. She gazed down upon Marietta, who looked awful—as if she had aged a hundred years during her nap. Even the clusters of grapes on her dress looked shriveled. Lionel, who had always looked that way, stood beside her, unchanged. Behind them both stood Sissy, who had kept herself admirably under control, Ivy thought, and next to Sissy, Veddy, crisp and at attention. Ray had abandoned his post in front of the cake and was staring up at Ivy, all ears.

Ivy kept everyone standing

for what she had to say. She waited to speak until the room felt dead serious. Then she began. "Marietta Noland," she said. "Marietta Noland," she said again. "I hereby find..." She paused and let the silence linger in the air, hang over them all, powerful as anything. And at last she cried out, loud and clear: "Dan and Carol *innocent*!"

What a beautiful word, *innocent*—a word right up there with *pergola*, and *intercepted*, and *traversing*; a word like music, like sugar on her tongue. *Innocent*: the one and only word Ivy had been dying to hear. She felt like she had been waiting her whole life to say it.

"And I sentence you to get them out and set them free."

At Ivy's decree Ray erupted in cheers and everyone else started buzzing: a lovely commotion, she thought; Ivy remembered how it had been in the courtroom, at her parents' trial. She remembered the roaring inside her head. And now, standing on the step, looking out over everyone, she felt a roaring again, but it wasn't one that cut out all the other sounds or things that were going on around her. She was on top of this roar, riding this sound that was like the whole world cheering, riding it like a wave that she knew would carry her far.

Meanwhile the murmuring down in the entryway built and then dissolved on its own. At last Ivy raised her hammer and gave the coaster a final, solid, satisfying whack. She descended the stairs, marched up to Marietta, and escorted her by her bony elbow into the library, over to the phone. "Call the judge," she ordered—the mustached one who had presided over Dan and Carol's trial—"and spring 'em."

Marietta started to stammer excuses. "But I couldn't *possibly*," she began. "*Quite* out of the question..." But her words faded; all her sentences came to nothing.

"Call," Ivy said, pointing to the phone.

It turned out that the judge was a relative, too—"but distant," Marietta sniffed. "From Lionel's side of the family." Still, she had his home phone number in her little black book and woke him up from a nap to insist there had been a miscarriage of justice. "I want to drop all charges," she told him, "in light of new evidence and information." She listened for a moment to whatever the judge had to say and then declared, "Oh, I don't care *how* you do it, George—just get them *out!*"

"Or *else!*" Ivy added, loud enough for everyone who was listening outside the door to hear.

Finally Marietta put the phone back in its cradle.

"Done and done," she told Ivy.

"What?" Ivy said. She wished Marietta talked more like Dan.

Marietta sighed. "Your parents' release," she said.

"A fait accompli."

Ivy made a face.

"It's all set," Marietta translated.

Then it was as if a thousand pounds had been lifted from Ivy's shoulders. She saw the backs of her parents' heads, every one of their sweet curls gleaming. She suddenly felt as light as air, ready to race her heart out. She and Ray would run the entire length of the hallway, East and West Wings both. She would fly. She would win every time.

Marietta was holding her back, though—she had reached out her bony hand and clasped Ivy's wrist. "But what shall become of *me*?" she quavered.

"You?" Ivy said.

"*Me!*" Marietta sang out, as if it were the diamond of words. "What shall become of *me*?" she repeated. "Must I throw myself on your mercy?"

"*What* mercy?" Ivy asked. She didn't know what Marietta was talking about. "The trial's over," she said, stating the obvious. "You lost."

"But you *won't* turn me over to the authorities, will you? Or banish me from my beloved home..." Marietta made a sweeping gesture back toward the grand entryway.

"Oh," Ivy said, nodding. She finally understood what Marietta was talking about. "You're afraid we'll send you up the river!"

Marietta gasped at even the mention of prison. Her whole skinny body was quivering.

Ivy leaned in closer to say what she had to say. "In *our* family," she began, her voice so filled with emotion that it had a little quaver to it, "we don't *rat* on each other." She gave a little stamp of her foot for emphasis. "We don't send people away. We don't even disown them."

What Ivy had to say sank in on both of them. Marietta let out a little yelp of relief; Ivy felt a twinge at the thought of never getting rid of Marietta.

"But things are gonna be different around here," she promised. "Ray and I are in charge now. With our own devices!"

Time Off for
Questionable Behavior

For most children in Hammerhill, September 4 marked the first day of school. But not for Ray and Ivy. They had declared September 4 a holiday in honor of Dan and Carol's official release from prison.

When she awoke that morning, Ivy climbed from her high bed onto the little footstool Sissy had placed below, and for just a moment her bare feet covered all the tiny stitches that spelled out *Where there's a will there's a way.* She skipped across to the bathroom and through it into Ray's old room. They had moved him back upstairs the first night after the trial, and Sissy had made up a bed fit for a king, piled high in silks and satins—and zapperless. Now Ivy watched him sleeping, his head resting on the embroidered pillow, with just the words *will* and *way* visible next to his profile.

She tiptoed in. "C'mon, Ray," Ivy said, bending over him. "Today's the day."

They had planned an especially delicious breakfast in honor of the upcoming event, and Ivy was hungry.

They went tripping down the grand staircase and hopscotched into the dining room. Lionel was already there, seated at the far end of the table. How he had perked up in the days immediately following the trial! On a number of occasions Ivy had come upon him in the library, relaxing in his electric chair, *chuckling*—she was sure of it.

Ray went and took a seat beside him. They were becoming buddies, of sorts. Lionel let Ray fool around with his magnifying glass and Ray was trying to make Lionel's newspaper at least start to smoke. There were plenty of rays to magnify because Ivy had pulled back the heavy brocade drapes and the room was drenched in sunlight. She and Veddy had also changed the decor: Marietta's portrait had been moved to an upstairs closet and replaced by the picture of Blackie Mutton, who now hung smirking over them all, as if he had had the last laugh.

Ivy seated herself at the head of the table, and then Veddy, who had taken to joining them for meals, entered and sat down beside her in Ivy's old place. He had become Ivy's right-hand man. With her hammer and coaster at the ready, she surveyed the long and lovely table spread out before her.

"I trust you slept well," she said to Veddy in greeting.

"Splendidly," he answered her.

She gave her first whack of the hammer and Sissy made her entrance through the swinging door. She had been crying—but for joy—ever since baby brother Luther (who turned out to be nearly seven feet tall) had arrived, and her face was a little puffy. She stepped back and held the door open wide.

In came Marietta, struggling a bit beneath a tray piled high with food. But the uniform that had always seemed too big on Sissy fit her like a glove.

"This will do quite nicely," Ivy called out, eyeing the platters and bowls coming their way—bacon and cereal and strawberries, whipped cream, chocolate

kisses. And a dozen hardboiled eggs, each in its own special holder. Veddy actually preferred eggs for breakfast; Ray and Ivy just liked using the clipper to chop off their tops.

At ten o'clock sharp Veddy brought the limo around,

and Ray and Ivy set off for prison to collect Carol and Dan. Sissy and Luther waved goodbye from the front porch, and Lionel waved, too, although not exactly in their direction. Marietta hadn't joined them; she was inside, on all fours, still scrubbing away at those nasty skidmarks in the entryway.

Ray and Ivy, meanwhile, were settling in for the ride. A spin in the limo on a beautiful day was always a pleasure. They sipped from cans of raspberry soda. They raised and lowered the window shades. The countryside sailed by. When, at one point, Broken Sparrow Academy came into view—high on the hill in the distance—Veddy tooted the horn and zoomed right on by.

"*That* was a narrow escape," Ivy said, eyeing the mansion and thinking how close they had come to being sent off there.

"Yeah," Ray agreed.

Ivy tilted her head back and took a long drink. "We did OK," she said. She was feeling pretty good about how things had turned out.

"Yeah," Ray agreed.

"Took care of business, got the lay of the land," she continued.

Ray nodded along.

"So when Carol asks," she said next, "be sure and tell her I watched your back."

"OK," Ray said. "And tell her I watched yours, too."

"Watched *mine*?" Ivy almost choked on her soda. And she was just about to set Ray straight when Veddy pulled up to the prison gate, and she saw them—Carol and Dan—standing in the sunlight, free.